He regarded her fo... id you've always bee... I can't change your m...

As you get used to life here and see how the tenants need guidance, you'll change your opinions."

She shook her head. "I wouldn't count on it." Her gaze softened, and she reached up and stroked his cheek. "I don't want to argue with you, Marcus. I love you with all my heart, and I want us to be happy. Please try to understand how I feel."

His heart pricked at the sadness he detected on her face. How could he deny her anything? "I want us to be happy, too. I love you so much, Victoria, but you have to understand you've entered a different world."

SANDRA ROBBINS and her husband live in the small college town where she grew up. Until a few years ago she was working as an elementary school principal, but God opened the door for her to become a full-time writer. Without the help of her wonderful husband, four children, and five grandchildren who have supported her dreams for many years, it would be impossible to write. As a child, Sandra accepted Jesus as her Savior and has depended on Him to guide her throughout her life. It is her prayer that God will use her words to plant seeds of hope in the lives of her readers. To find out more about Sandra and her books, go to her website at http://sandrarobbins.net.

Books by Sandra Robbins

HEARTSONG PRESENTS
HP919—The Columns of Cottonwood
HP940—Dinner at the St. James

Blues Along the River

Sandra Robbins

Heartsong Presents

This book is dedicated to the memory of my wonderful father, who bought me my first piano and started me on a lifelong appreciation for all types of music. I miss playing for you, Daddy.

A note from the Author:
I love to hear from my readers! You may correspond with me by writing:

Sandra Robbins
Author Relations
PO Box 721
Uhrichsville, OH 44683

ISBN 978-1-61626-368-3

BLUES ALONG THE RIVER

All scripture quotations are taken from the King James Version of the Bible.

All of the characters and events in this book are fictitious. Any resemblance to actual persons, living or dead, or to actual events is purely coincidental.

Our mission is to publish and distribute inspirational products offering exceptional value and biblical encouragement to the masses.

PRINTED IN THE U.S.A.

one

The whistle of the *Alabama Maiden* pierced the afternoon quiet. Victoria Turner stopped in her stroll along the deck of the steamboat and peered toward the riverbank to her right. Two boys, each holding a fishing pole, jumped up from the ground, grabbed the straw hats from their heads, and waved to the passing boat.

Victoria leaned against the railing and waved in return. The wake of the ship rippled across the surface of the Alabama River and washed across the boys' bare feet on the shore.

She turned to her mother, who had stopped beside her, and pointed toward the edge of the water. "Look, those boys are barefooted already, and it's only the first of May. They must be looking forward to summer."

Her mother laughed and waved to the boys. "The days are getting warmer. I always loved spring when I was growing up in central Alabama. This is the time of year when the farmers prepare their fields for planting. In fact, they may already have a lot of their cotton planted."

Victoria cast one more glance at the boys and let her gaze wander up the bluff behind them. The thick green leaves on the trees rustled in the warm breeze that blew from the river. The memory of the tall oak tree in their backyard in Mobile flashed in her mind, and she blinked back tears. She wished she could be sitting under it right now.

The azalea bush outside the parlor window in their house would be in full bloom by now. Each spring since she was a young child, she'd watched every day to get a glimpse of the first blossom to appear. This year someone else would enjoy the deep pink flowers she loved. She'd be living above a general store on the main street of a small river town, miles from the only world she'd ever known.

"Oh look, there's another one!" Her mother grabbed the steamship deck railing with one hand and pointed with the other to the top of the bluff and the white-columned plantation home that gleamed in the sunlight.

It was the third mansion they had seen on their journey upriver from Mobile to Willow Bend. Victoria's breath caught in her throat at the sight. "It's the most beautiful one yet," she whispered.

Victoria had never seen anything like it. Six colonnades towered across the front of the two-story house, and a cupola with a walkway around it sat on the roof. She could imagine a large veranda with a table and comfortable chairs for relaxing and sipping cool drinks on the rear of the house.

Her mother stared in the direction of the house and nodded. "I remember going to a dinner there when your father and I came to visit my brother years ago. The man who owned it was a friend of his. I don't remember his name, though."

"May I be of assistance to you ladies?"

Victoria glanced over her shoulder and smiled. "Captain Mills, I didn't hear you come up behind us."

The white beard and mustache that covered the man's face wiggled as his mouth curved into a friendly smile that he directed toward her mother. "I hope I didn't startle you,

Mrs. Turner. I was coming along the deck and thought there might be some way I could be of help."

Victoria covered her mouth with the handkerchief she held to hide her smile. Ever since they had boarded the *Alabama Maiden* in Mobile, Captain Mills had been very attentive to her mother. Although she insisted that he treated all his passengers the same, her mother appeared to be enjoying the man's attention.

Victoria pointed to the plantation home on the bluff. "We were just admiring that beautiful house. Mama was a guest there once, but she's forgotten the owner's name."

Captain Mills stood straight with his shoulders back and his hands clasped behind his back. He nodded toward the towering mansion. "That's the big house of Pembrook Plantation."

Victoria stared at the imposing structure. A door in the center of the second floor opened onto a balcony that ran the length of the front of the house. She couldn't help but compare the mansion's size with the small house she and her mother had shared in Mobile. Theirs would probably fit in one corner of the structure. "With its size, it's no wonder they call it the big house."

Captain Mills chuckled. "No matter how large or small, the planters have always referred to the main plantation home as the big house. It doesn't have so much to do with size as it does the symbol of authority the house reflects. Pembrook's big house is indeed one of the most beautiful along the river. The former owner's name was Sebastian Raines. He died a few years ago, and now his son, Marcus, runs the plantation."

Her mother nodded. "Oh yes, I remember now. Mr. Raines and his son, who was a small child at the time, lived there when my brother took us for a visit." Her forehead wrinkled in thought. "That must have been at least twenty-five years ago."

Victoria studied the mansion as the steamboat plowed on through the Alabama River waters and left the big house of Pembrook behind. She wondered what it would be like to live in a house like that. There had to be servants who catered to the residents' needs. Not like the life she and her mother had lived in the year since her father's death. They had barely scraped by on the money Victoria had earned working in the kitchen of a boardinghouse in Mobile.

She glanced down at her red hands and curled her fingers into her palms. She'd scrubbed more pots and pans in the last year than she could count, but at least she'd been in Mobile, where there were lots of people, not in a small river landing town like Willow Bend in the middle of Alabama's Black Belt. There might be a lot of large plantations around, but her only hope of ever seeing the inside of one of those houses was if she ended up working in one of their kitchens.

"So you're going to live with your brother in Willow Bend?" Captain Mills's voice caught Victoria's attention.

"We are," her mother replied. "He lives above the general store he owns in Willow Bend. He has an extra bedroom that Victoria and I can share, and I'll keep house for him. Victoria will help out in the store when she's needed. I think we're going to enjoy living in a small town after the hustle and bustle of Mobile."

Victoria's heart sank at her mother's words. Her mother might look forward to life in Willow Bend, but Victoria couldn't imagine anything more depressing. She'd lived in the city all her life, and there was nothing that would make her like the little river town.

Her mother had told her she would probably meet some

young women her own age at church. She didn't want new friends. No one could take the place of Margaret and Clara, who had been her friends ever since she could remember. The three of them had shared childhood secrets, and for the past few years their main topic of conversation had been the men they would marry. Now she was miles away from the friends who seemed more like sisters, and she'd never felt more alone.

She closed her eyes and tried to banish the vision that had occupied her mind ever since her mother announced they were going to live with her uncle. The years would drift by with her working in the town's general store, and before she knew it, she would be an old maid who no man would have an interest in marrying.

Captain Mills glanced in Victoria's direction. "Tell me, Miss Turner, have you visited Willow Bend before?"

"Once when I was a child. I remember the landing where the paddle wheelers docked and the main street that ran along the river bluff. My uncle's store faced the river, and there were a few more businesses. A livery stable, I think, but I don't remember the others."

Captain Mills laughed. "That's about all that's there now. The church and the school are on the outskirts of town."

Victoria's heart sank at the man's words. She'd hoped that Willow Bend had grown since she'd last visited, but it hadn't. She sighed. "It doesn't sound like there's much activity."

"Oh, on the contrary. The congregation at the church has really grown in the last few years. I hear it's because the people in the region have such respect for the pastor. His name is Daniel Luckett, and his wife's name is Tave. She's not much older than you, Miss Turner. She'll take you under her wing and introduce you to all the young people in the community."

For the first time since her journey to Willow Bend began,

Victoria felt a sliver of hope. Maybe she would meet some people who could make her exile to Willow Bend more tolerable.

She glanced back downriver, but Pembrook's big house had disappeared from view. With a sigh, she pushed away from the railing. "How long before we dock?"

"About thirty minutes." Captain Mills turned back to her mother, and his gaze raked her face. "I hope you've enjoyed your trip upriver with us, Mrs. Turner. I'll have one of the deck hands take your luggage to your brother's store when we arrive. In the meantime, if you need anything, please let me know."

Her mother's face flushed. "Thank you, Captain Mills. You've been very attentive to our needs, and we appreciate it."

He bowed slightly, turned, and strode down the deck. Victoria watched him go before she looped her arm through her mother's and guided her back toward their cabin. "I think you've got an admirer, Mama, and I have to say I really like him."

Her mother waved a hand in dismissal. "Captain Mills is just being helpful. We'll probably never see him again after we leave the ship."

At their cabin door, Victoria glanced over her shoulder and caught a glimpse of the captain staring at them from the far end of the deck. When he saw her look at him, he whirled and disappeared around the end of the walkway to the other side of the ship. With a chuckle Victoria shook her head. "I wouldn't be too sure about that."

Her mother opened the door to the cabin and turned to direct a stern glare in Victoria's direction. "Quit teasing and come make sure you have everything in the trunk before we close it. We'll be landing at our new home in a few minutes."

Victoria paused in the doorway and winced. "Home? I

doubt if I'll ever feel that way about Willow Bend."

Her mother's shoulders slumped as she sat on the edge of the bed. "Victoria, you know there was nothing else we could do. The small amount of money you made at that boardinghouse didn't start to cover our living expenses. We've used up everything your father left. We're fortunate my brother is willing to help us."

Victoria fought back the tears that threatened to fill her eyes. "I understand, and I promised I would make the best of the situation for your sake. But I want more out of life than being an unmarried woman living with my mother and uncle over the store where I work."

Her mother held out her hand. Victoria grasped it and sat beside her. "You're young, and it's natural you should worry about what life has in store for you. I was the same way when I was your age, but things worked out for me. I met your father, and one of these days you're going to meet a nice young man, too."

Victoria gave a snort of disgust. "In a little river town in the middle of Alabama? I doubt it."

Her mother smiled. "You never can tell what the future holds."

The boat's whistle rumbled, and Victoria pushed up from the bed. "We're almost there. We'd better get the trunk ready." She glanced at her mother, who still sat on the bed. "Don't worry, Mama. I'm thankful that Uncle Samuel is willing to offer us a place to live, and I've come with you. I've told you from the beginning, though, that I don't expect to be there long."

Her mother shook her head. "Ever since you were a child, you've been so impulsive. Be careful, darling. The things that look so good on the outside can sometimes contain the biggest flaws on the inside."

Victoria stared at her mother for a moment before she stepped to the trunk to prepare for her arrival in Willow Bend.

❧

Marcus Raines hopped down from the seat of the wagon the minute James Moses pulled the horses to a stop in front of Perkins General Store. He pulled the straw hat from his head and wiped at the perspiration on his forehead. The last month had been hotter than usual for this time of year, but that had been good. It had given him the time needed to get the fields ready for spring planting and some of the cotton in the ground. If his new purchases arrived on today's boat, the tenant farmers at Pembrook ought to have the entire cotton crop planted by the end of next week.

He squinted up at the young man who still sat on the wagon seat, the reins in his hands. James kept his gaze directed toward his feet and didn't move to wipe at the sweat that covered his chocolate-colored skin. Neither of them had spoken on the drive into town, and Marcus wondered what the young man, the son of one of his tenant farmers, was thinking. His facial expression gave no hint of what went on behind James's dark eyes, which never focused on Marcus.

But then, Marcus had no idea what any of the tenant farmers thought. The ones who'd been slaves before the war regarded him as if he was the enemy at times, and others appeared to tolerate him as the owner of the land they farmed. He wished he had a relationship with his tenant farmers like the one Dante Rinaldi had at Cottonwood, but he didn't know how to go about getting it.

Ever since his father's death, Marcus had tried to get his tenant farmers to treat him the same way they had his father, but it was no use. His father had ruled Pembrook with an iron hand, and he knew how to deal with the men who farmed his land. None of them ever approached his father unless they held their hat in their hand and spoke with respect. For some reason, he hadn't been able to teach Marcus the secret to wielding power on the large plantation.

Marcus had agonized over the problem for many sleepless nights, but a solution hadn't presented itself yet. Perhaps he was the one at fault, for he had never learned the art of conversation. As a child, he'd lived in isolation on the plantation with his father and had only known the tutors his father had hired to educate him. He'd never had a friend, and no woman had ever given him more than a passing glance. How he wished he could laugh and talk with his neighbors like Dante did, but he never felt as if he had anything worthwhile to add to the conversation.

With a sigh, Marcus walked away from the wagon and headed toward the landing where the paddle wheelers docked on their way up and down the river. The whistle of the *Alabama Maiden* pierced the air, and he smiled. He turned and called out to James. "The boat's coming around the bend. Go on down to the landing and be ready to help unload those cotton planters I ordered."

Without speaking, James set the wagon brake and climbed down. After tying the reins to a hitching post, he walked down the bluff to the landing.

Behind him, Marcus heard footsteps as the people of Willow Bend hurried to the landing intent on seeing the big ship dock at their little town. Fewer steamboats plowed the river now than when Marcus was a boy. Soon, he suspected, the railroad, with its faster means of transportation, would spell the doom of the beautiful ships he'd watched from the bluff in front of his home all his life.

"Good afternoon, Marcus. Are you meeting someone on the boat?"

Marcus turned at the sound of a man's voice beside him. Samuel Perkins, the owner of the general store, peered at him over the rims of the spectacles that rested on the bridge of his nose. Marcus shook his head. "No. I'm expecting some cotton planters that I ordered from Mobile."

Mr. Perkins shoved his hands in the pockets of his pants and rocked back on his heels. "Dante Rinaldi was in the store the other day. He said he bought some last year. Are yours like the ones he has?"

Marcus nodded. "They are. My father never would buy any. He said he liked to see men in the fields planting. But from what Dante says, a man using one of those plow-type cotton planters can plant eight acres of cotton in a day. Planting that much by hand takes at least ten to fifteen men."

Mr. Perkins cocked an eyebrow and stared at Marcus. "Your pa didn't like change. Wanted everything to stay the way it was. I'm glad to see you're trying to farm more efficiently. You listen to Dante. When he bought Cottonwood after the war, nobody around here thought he'd make it profitable again, but he did. Now it grows some of the best cotton and corn in Alabama. You're gonna do the same with Pembrook."

Marcus's face flushed. "I don't know about that."

"Well, it sounds to me like. . ." Mr. Perkins paused and pointed to the big ship that glided around the bend. "There she is. I guess they finally made it."

"They?" Marcus turned a questioning glance toward the man.

Mr. Perkins laughed. "Haven't you heard? I'm gaining two new family members today. My sister's husband died a year ago, and she and her daughter are arriving from Mobile to live with me. They've had a hard time since my brother-in-law's death."

Marcus hoped his face conveyed a sympathetic look as he turned to stare at the ship that eased up to the landing at the base of the bluff. He caught sight of James, who stood talking to Henry Walton, one of the tenant farmers from Cottonwood. Henry laughed at something James said and slapped him on the back.

Henry was one of the few white tenant farmers in the area, but he was accepted by all the others, some of whom had been former slaves. Marcus wondered about Henry's secret to having a good relationship with all the other farmers. Maybe sometime he'd get up his courage and ask the man.

"There they are!" Mr. Perkins's excited voice cut through Marcus's thoughts.

He glanced in the direction the store owner pointed and spotted two women standing at the railing of the deck. He knew there were two women because Mr. Perkins said so, but the vision of only one penetrated his mind.

She wore a blue traveling dress with a jacket that reached below her knees and a hat made of the same material as the coat. The ribbons dangling from the hat had been tied between her throat and ear on the left side of her face, and the jaunty bow rippled in the breeze. Dark hair stuck out from under the hat, and she stood on deck like a queen. He'd never seen anyone more beautiful in his life.

"Wh—what is your niece's name?" Marcus frowned at the stammer in his voice.

"Victoria. Victoria Turner." Mr. Perkins turned to him. "That's my sister, Ellen, beside her. I'll introduce you to them with they come ashore."

Marcus glanced at Mr. Perkins's sister before he let his gaze settle once again on the niece. *Victoria.* The name sent a tingle of pleasure through him. It sounded like it might belong to an angel.

As he watched, Victoria waved, and Marcus raised his hand to respond until he realized the greeting was for her uncle, not for him. Embarrassed and fearful someone had witnessed his blunder, he glanced around. No one appeared to be paying any attention to him.

The crew on the ship lowered the gangplank, and the passengers began to come ashore. He didn't move as he watched her follow her mother onto the bank and hurry up the bluff toward her uncle. When she reached Mr. Perkins, she waited while her mother and uncle embraced before she stepped forward and gave her uncle a quick hug.

"Uncle Samuel, it's so good to see you." The lilting drawl of her words made his pulse race.

Mr. Perkins pointed to him. "Ellen, Victoria, I'd like to introduce you to Mr. Marcus Raines of Pembrook Plantation. Mr. Raines, my sister and niece."

Marcus pulled off his hat and held it in front of him. "Mrs. Turner, your brother told me that you were coming here to live. I hope you enjoy Willow Bend."

She nodded. "I'm sure we will, Mr. Raines." She glanced at her daughter. "This is Victoria. I'm afraid she's not as happy as I am about our move to this small town."

Dark eyes bored into his soul when he turned back to the young woman. He swallowed and tried to speak. "Miss Turner, I'm sure you'll like living here. There are many young women who'll help make you feel at home."

She smiled, and his heart flipped. "Thank you, Mr. Raines. So you're the owner of Pembrook? We saw your house from the boat. Mama says she was a guest there years ago."

His eyes widened. "Is that right? Well, you must come again."

Victoria stepped closer to him. "Mama and I would love to meet your wife."

His face grew warm, and he gave a nervous laugh. "I'm afraid that won't be possible since I'm not married. But I'd still like for you to visit my home."

A smile curled her lips, and she tilted her head to one side. "We would be delighted."

At that moment, he caught sight of James and several deck hands bringing his cotton planters up the bluff. He backed away and put the hat back on his head. "I'm afraid I have to be going now. It was nice to meet you, Mrs. Turner. And you, too, Miss Turner."

He started to turn and head up the bluff, but she called out to him. "Captain Mills told us about the church and the pastor and his wife. Mama and I will be attending on Sunday. Maybe we'll see you there also."

Marcus stopped, uncertain what to say. His father hadn't been a believer and had never seen the need to take his son to church. Marcus had never been to the Willow Bend Church and had no idea what went on inside the building. A sudden thought struck him—he wanted to be there if Victoria Turner would be in the congregation.

He smiled. "I'll see you then."

The look of surprise on Mr. Perkins's face sent guilt flowing through him. Who was he trying to fool? He hadn't been brought up to be a churchgoer, and he had no desire to become one now.

A lot of pretty women lived along the river of west central Alabama, and he'd never given a thought to any of them.

How could a woman he'd barely spoken with make him want to attend church when he'd never wanted to before?

He shook his head and hurried toward the wagon where James waited. Before he climbed in, he glanced over his shoulder. Victoria, her hand in the crook of her uncle's arm, glided across the street toward the store. She glanced in his direction, smiled, and gave a slight nod.

Marcus tipped his hat and climbed into the wagon. He didn't know what had happened to him today, but he did know one thing. There was no need to waste his time thinking about Victoria Turner. Their brief meeting at the dock would probably be the only conversation they'd ever have.

two

Two mornings later, Victoria leaned against the sales counter in her uncle's store and blew at a stray strand of hair that dangled in front of her eyes. "Is it always this busy on Saturday mornings?"

Her uncle chuckled and picked up the bolt of cloth he'd cut some yardage from for a customer earlier and walked to the table where the dress goods were displayed. "Most folks around here try to get to town on Saturdays. If you think this morning's been busy, the afternoon will be worse. That's when the farmers load up their families and drive into town. By noon you'll see wagons and buggies tied up all along the main street, and children will run in and out of here all afternoon."

Victoria opened her mouth to express her apprehension, but a sudden thought struck her. Smiling, she turned to her uncle. "All the farmers? Do you think the owner of Pembrook will come?"

Her uncle lay the bolt down and shook his head. "I doubt it. Marcus Raines is a private person, a loner you might say. He hardly ever comes into town. If he needs something from the store, he sends Sally Moses. Her husband's a tenant farmer on Pembrook, and Sally is the housekeeper in the big house."

Disappointment surged through Victoria. She hadn't been able to get the man out of her mind ever since she'd met him the day she arrived, and she couldn't understand it. If she'd passed him on the street, she probably wouldn't have noticed him, although she had to admit he was quite handsome. That wasn't the only thing about him that appealed to her, though. He was also wealthy and unmarried.

But one thing about him puzzled her. There was a vulnerability that radiated from his deep blue eyes. Even the way he stood with his hat in his hand had given the image of someone unsure of himself. She couldn't imagine why he would feel that way. After all, he was the owner of a grand plantation.

With a sigh she picked up the feather duster from a shelf behind the sales counter. She was being silly trying to analyze a man she'd only seen once and might not see again for a long time if what Uncle Samuel said was true.

She turned to the display shelves along the wall and had taken one swipe with the duster when the bell above the front door jingled. She turned to see a young woman coming in the door.

Her uncle looked up from rearranging the bolts of cloth and smiled. "Good morning, Tave. I thought it was about time you came in. I can almost set my watch on Saturday mornings by your arrival."

The woman laughed and stopped next to him. "I'm a little late today. I had to go by my father's office." She glanced across the room and spied Victoria. A big smile curled her lips, and she hurried forward. "You must be Victoria. Your uncle has told me all about you. I'm Tave Luckett."

The name sounded familiar. Victoria searched her mind and then smiled. "You're the wife of the pastor at the church. Captain Mills told us about you and your husband when we were on the boat. We're looking forward to coming to church tomorrow."

Tave smiled. "Good. Everybody is excited to meet you and

your mother. We want to make you feel welcome in Willow Bend."

For the first time since coming to Willow Bend, Victoria felt a sense of relief. Maybe it wasn't going to be as bad here as she had thought. If everyone was as friendly as Tave, there might be hope for finding some friendships in the small town.

"Are there any unmarried young women my age who live nearby?"

Tave thought for a minute. "We have a few. Becky Thompson isn't married yet, but she's engaged. Also Katherine Wainscott over at Oak Hill Plantation is still home with her parents." Tave's eyes lit up, and she glanced over her shoulder. "Mr. Perkins, I have an idea. We need to have some kind of gathering to introduce your sister and niece to all the people around here."

Victoria's heart pumped. "Oh, that sounds wonderful."

Her uncle walked back to where they stood and frowned. "No need to do that. They'll meet everybody soon enough."

The bewildered look on her uncle's face sent Victoria's hopes crashing down. Before she could say anything, Tave patted her uncle's arm and laughed. "Men usually don't understand a woman's need to make friends quickly. With the good weather we're having, everybody's been talking about how it's almost time for a dinner after church. We'll announce it at church tomorrow and have the dinner next week." She glanced back at Victoria. "How does that sound?"

"It sounds wonderful."

Tave nodded. "We can eat after church and spend the afternoon visiting. We don't get the opportunity to do that very often. And you can meet everybody from all the plantations and farms."

A thought struck Victoria. "I've already met one person

who I hope will come."

"Who's that?"

"Marcus Raines. He was at the landing when Mama and I got off the boat."

Tave and her uncle exchanged quick glances. "I don't know if I'd count on that," Tave said.

Victoria felt her eyes grow wide. "Why not?"

"Marcus doesn't attend our church. My husband has tried to get him to come, but he won't. He keeps to himself and doesn't encourage friendships."

Victoria glanced at her uncle. "Why not, Uncle Samuel? Is there something wrong with him?"

Her uncle cleared his throat. "I've only had dealings with him in the store, and he's always been fair and paid his bills. But a lot of the farmers don't like him. They think he sees himself as better than they are."

Victoria shook her head. "I didn't think that at all when we met."

"I think he's just shy and unsure of himself," Tave added. "But it doesn't make any difference, because I doubt he would come."

"Maybe he would if your husband asked him again." Victoria hoped she didn't sound like she was pleading.

Tave shrugged. "I'll tell him to, but don't be disappointed if he doesn't show up."

The more she heard, the more her hopes that she would get to know the handsome owner of Pembrook were dashed. He was probably just being polite when he said she and her mother must visit his home sometime.

The bell over the door jingled, and the three of them turned to see who had entered. Victoria's breath caught in her throat at the sight of Marcus Raines standing just inside the door. He wasn't dressed in the work clothes he'd had on the last time she'd seen him. Today he wore a pair of high-cut black trousers that accented his small waist. A pair of suspenders stretched over his white shirt emphasized his broad shoulders. He pulled a wide-brimmed black felt hat from his head and held it in front of him.

His gaze flitted over the group before it came to rest on the store owner, who cleared his throat and stepped forward. "Marcus, what a surprise. I expected to see Sally today. She usually does your shopping."

Marcus nodded. "I know, but I told her I'd do it today." He took a deep breath before he fumbled in his pants pocket, pulled out a piece of paper, and held it out. "Here's the list of things I need."

Her uncle scanned the items. "Most of this stuff is in the storeroom. I'll get it for you. Victoria will help you with anything else you need."

As her uncle left the room, Victoria could only stare at the man she'd met a few days ago. He was even handsomer than she remembered. She finally managed a smile. "It's good to see you again, Mr. Raines."

He bit his lip and nodded before he glanced at Tave. "It's nice to see you, too. And you, Mrs. Luckett."

Tave smiled. "I just came in to meet Victoria." She sucked in her breath and frowned. "Oh, I left my list over at my father's office. I'll go get it and come back later." She turned to Victoria. "I'm glad you're living here, and I can hardly wait to get started on the plans for the church dinner."

When the door closed behind Tave, Marcus eased across the floor in Victoria's direction. "Mrs. Luckett's father is the town doctor. His name is Dr. Spencer."

"I didn't know that."

The brim of his hat curled as his fingers tightened on it. "Are you settled in your new home yet, Miss Turner?"

Victoria moved back behind the counter and smiled. "Almost." When he didn't say anything else, she placed her hands on the counter and leaned forward. "Is there something else I can help you with?"

He shook his head. "I don't think so." He licked his lips. "It's good to see you again."

"I'm glad to see you, too. Tave and I were just talking about you. She said you don't attend the Willow Bend Church."

"I don't."

"Have you ever been?"

"No."

"Do you think you might not like it?"

He shrugged. "I suppose I've never thought about it much. My father didn't see the need of attending church, and I never have, either."

His words struck a warning in her heart. Her father had seen to it that she and her mother attended church every Sunday. Since her father's death, they hadn't gone as regularly, but her mother had already told her that the church in Willow Bend would be their best opportunity to socialize in the tiny community. If Victoria was to make friends, she'd find them there. "Maybe if you came, you'd find out differently. And you did tell me at the dock the day I arrived that you would see me at church."

His eyebrows arched, and a smile tugged at the corners of his mouth. "You're right. I really shouldn't go back on my word. So I suppose I'll see you tomorrow."

She smiled. "I'm glad. You know you're the first person I met here, and I hope we can be friends."

He shoved his hands in his pockets. "Maybe we can. I don't have many friends."

Victoria almost gasped aloud as she stared into Marcus's blue eyes. Loneliness flickered in their depths. "Then we have to do something about that. The church is going to have a dinner next Sunday to introduce my mother and me to the community. I hope you'll come then, too."

He hesitated a moment. "I don't know. . . ."

She held up a hand to silence him. "I won't take no for an answer."

His Adam's apple bobbed. "Do you want me to come, Miss Turner?"

Victoria arched an eyebrow. "Mr. Raines, did you not hear me say I hope you'll come? I wouldn't have said it if I hadn't meant it." Her mouth curled into a smile. "I expect to see you there."

"Then I'll be there, Miss Turner."

"Good." She inhaled. "Now one more thing. If we're going to be friends, I want you to call me Victoria. *Miss Turner* makes me sound like an old woman."

His gaze flitted over her. "You're certainly not old. If I'm to call you Victoria, then you must call me Marcus."

She smiled. "It's nice to have a friend in Willow Bend."

"I agree."

At that moment Victoria's uncle reappeared from the back of the store. "I have everything you need at the loading dock out back. You can pull your wagon around there, and I'll help you load it."

Marcus shook his head. "There's no need for that. James and I will get it." He turned toward Victoria. "It's good to see you, Victoria. I'm looking forward to church tomorrow and attending the dinner next Sunday."

"And I am, too, Marcus."

"You're coming to church tomorrow?" Her uncle's voice held a hint of surprise.

Marcus smiled. "Yes. Maybe it's time I got to know my neighbors better. I'll see you then." Without another word, he whirled and hurried toward the door.

When Marcus left the store, Victoria's uncle turned to stare at her with wide eyes. "That was quite a surprise."

A surge of energy shot through Victoria. She hadn't felt so happy in years. "I don't know why you and Tave think he's so strange. I like him very much."

Her uncle reached out and put a restraining hand on her arm. "I said that the other farmers feel he thinks he's better than they are. I doubt if anybody knows him well. That's what concerns me. You're a beautiful young woman, and I only want the best friends for you. Don't be swayed by the fact that he's wealthy. Make sure you choose friends who have the same beliefs your parents have instilled in you."

She laughed and patted her uncle's hand. "Don't worry. Besides Tave Luckett, he's the only person I've met in Willow Bend."

"I'm just telling you to be careful around Marcus."

"I will. Now I'm going to finish dusting before the afternoon customers get here."

She hurried across the room in order to distance herself from her uncle. His warning about Marcus lingered in her mind. Her father also had cautioned her many times about choosing friends who shared her belief in God. Even if Marcus had never attended church, that didn't mean he was an unbeliever. Perhaps her uncle's concerns were unfounded.

At the moment she didn't want to think about that. She wanted to recall how the handsome owner of Pembrook

Plantation had stared at her. She didn't understand why Marcus Raines stirred her heart, but he did. He reminded her of a small boy who needed someone to offer comfort. From what, she didn't know, but she intended to find out.

૨ૐ

Marcus Raines strode down the street toward the hitching post where he'd left James with the wagon. He clenched his fists as he walked and tried to make some sense out of what he'd just done. He'd never had any desire to attend church, and now he had committed to two Sundays and a dinner afterward.

When he'd gotten out of bed this morning, he'd known he couldn't wait until tomorrow to see Victoria Turner again. Sally Moses had looked surprised when he'd announced at breakfast that he would go to town in her place today. She hadn't tried to dissuade him. Instead, she had told him what she needed, and he'd made note of it.

All the way to town, he'd asked himself if he should have come. He'd almost backed out of stepping into that store, but when he opened the door and saw her standing there, he knew he'd made the right decision. She was even more beautiful than he remembered. He hadn't dared hope that he would get the opportunity to speak with her alone, but he had. He usually became tongue-tied when he talked with a young woman, but it hadn't been that way with Victoria. He had said more to her than any other woman he could remember.

Not only had they talked, but she had also invited him to a dinner in her honor. Then the best thing of all had happened. She had asked him to be her friend. When he answered her that he, too, was glad to have a friend in Willow Bend, he knew she had no idea what he meant. In truth, she was the first friend he'd ever had, and the thought made his heart pump.

The image of his father flashed in his mind and sent his good mood plummeting. His father had told him often enough that he should stay away from women. They couldn't be trusted. But there was something about Victoria that made Marcus question his father's words. He shared some kind of connection with the woman with the dark eyes. He doubted anything would ever come of it, though. When she got to know him better, she would find a reason to keep her distance from him.

three

As soon as the last prayer was said on Sunday morning, Marcus made a dash for the back door of the church, but he was too late. Pastor Daniel Luckett and his wife, Tave, had beaten him up the aisle. They must have quietly slipped to the back when the man in the front row was saying the benediction.

His plan had been to escape to the yard where his horse was tied and wait for Victoria and her family to come outside. Then he would go and speak to them, but the truth was that he was scared to death.

All through the sermon from three rows behind her, he had stared at the woman he hadn't been able to get out of his mind. He couldn't concentrate on what the preacher was saying for worrying that when he spoke to her after church, he wouldn't be able to carry on an intelligent conversation. What if she thought him dull and boring?

The crowd jostled him from behind, and he glanced around to see if there was another exit from the church, but it didn't matter. His retreat was blocked by people coming up the aisle behind him. Perspiration popped out on his head, and he pulled a handkerchief from his pocket to wipe it away. In front of him the pastor greeted his congregation with a smile and soft-spoken words.

It wasn't that he minded speaking to Reverend Luckett and his wife, but he didn't want anyone to make a fuss over the fact that he had come to church today. Maybe they would welcome him and let it go at that.

The pastor smiled and extended his hand as Marcus stopped in front of him. "Marcus," he said, "I've been praying for this day for a long time. It's so good to have you with us today."

Marcus grasped the man's hand. "Thank you."

"I hope you'll come again," Tave Luckett said before her gaze flitted over his shoulder.

Before he could respond, a voice behind him set his heart to pumping. "Not only did he come today, but he's coming next Sunday for the dinner."

Marcus turned and stared into Victoria Turner's face. His heart skipped a beat at how beautiful she looked today. He wanted to say something, but his mind had suddenly gone blank.

After a moment, Tave cleared her throat. "That's even more wonderful, Marcus. We'll look forward to seeing you then."

Marcus pulled his attention back to the pastor and his wife. "Thank you."

Reverend Luckett smiled. "Have a good day, Marcus."

Marcus offered a weak smile before he hurried to the rack across the back wall of the church and grabbed his hat. On the porch, he took a deep breath and glanced around at the people climbing into buggies and wagons. No one appeared to be paying any attention to him, and he relaxed. He made it to the bottom of the steps before his escape was halted by a familiar voice.

"Marcus, don't rush off before I get a chance to welcome you to church."

He turned to see Dante Rinaldi, his young son in tow, coming around the corner of the building. Of all the planters in the area, Marcus liked and respected Dante most. The man had come to Willow Bend a few years after the war, bought Cottonwood Plantation when it was in ruins, and restored it to the grand plantation it once had been. Considered an interloper at first, he was now one of the most respected residents in the Black Belt.

Marcus placed his hat on his head and waited for Dante to approach. There was a quality about Dante Rinaldi that Marcus envied. He seemed so sure of himself, and in all the years he'd known him, Marcus had never seen him lose his temper. When Dante and his son stopped beside him, the man glanced down at the young boy who Marcus thought must be about six or seven years old. Dirt smudged the boy's face and pants, and his shirttail hung over the waist of his pants.

Dante grinned down at the boy. "I had to break up a misunderstanding, and I was afraid you'd be gone before I got back to the front of the church."

Marcus shook his head. "No, I was waiting to speak to Mr. Perkins and his family."

Dante's smile grew bigger. "I'm glad you came today, Marcus. I've told you that you need to get out and meet people. You've stayed cooped up on that plantation all your life. You need to see what goes on outside of Pembrook. I think going to church and meeting people is a good start for you." He glanced toward the front door of the church and nodded to his son. "You'd better watch out. Here comes your mother."

Savannah Rinaldi stepped from the church with Victoria beside her. As they came down the steps, Savannah smiled at Marcus. "Victoria and I were discussing the dinner next Sunday. She tells me that you—" Her eyes narrowed as she caught sight of her son. "Vance Rinaldi, have you been fighting again?"

The boy hung his head and dug his toe into the dirt. "Yes, Mama."

Savannah grabbed a handkerchief from her reticule, wet it with her tongue, and scrubbed at the boy's face. "What am I going to do with you?" When she'd rubbed most of the dirt away, she held him at arms' length and scowled. "Go get in the buggy and wait for us. Your father and I will deal with you when we get home." The boy ran toward the buggy, and Savannah turned back to Marcus. "I'm glad to see you at church, Marcus. Please come again. Now if all of you will excuse me, I think we need to get home—that is, if I can find my daughter."

When she'd hurried off in search of the girl, Dante turned to Marcus and Victoria. "I guess I'd better go. Have a nice afternoon."

Dante strode toward the buggy where a dejected Vance sat. "I'm afraid Vance is in trouble," Marcus said.

Victoria laughed. "I think you're right, but Savannah and Dante seem like nice people."

"Oh, they are. My father met Dante soon after he came here. Most of the people didn't like him, and my father didn't for a long time. But he's a good man." Marcus watched Dante help his wife and daughter into the buggy and then pull out to the road. He'd always envied families that appeared happy, and Dante's family certainly did.

"What are you thinking?" Victoria's voice startled him.

He jerked his attention back to her. "Nothing." He let his gaze drift over her. "It's good to see you again, Victoria."

"It's good to see you, too. Thank you, Marcus."

He frowned. "For what?"

She smiled, and his heart raced. "For making me feel so welcome in Willow Bend. I really dreaded coming here. I didn't think I'd have any friends. Then I got off the boat, and you were standing there as if you'd come to welcome me. I knew we were going to be friends."

He wanted to respond, but the words wouldn't come, especially when he looked into Victoria's eyes. He silently berated himself.

Ducking his head, he nodded. "I have to be going. Maybe I'll see you this week."

Before she could respond, Marcus strode to where he'd tied his horse, mounted, and turned toward home. He glanced back at Victoria, who stared after him from the church yard. She had seemed happy to see him, but he couldn't think of anything to say. Anger flared within him, and he dug his heels into the horse's side.

Dante was right. He needed to get out and meet people. When he was a boy, his father had company all the time, but Marcus had always been banished to the upstairs and not allowed to listen to adult conversation.

By the time he'd reached his teens, his father wasn't well, and company at Pembrook became a thing of the past. Even though his father suffered from poor health for years, he ran Pembrook as if he would always be there. When Father died, Marcus realized he hadn't been prepared for the responsibility he'd inherited. Ever since he'd become the master of the plantation, he'd struggled to find his way and keep the land productive.

Now a woman he'd met only a week ago made him want something more than his lonely life at Pembrook. It surprised him that he had enjoyed being in the group of people at church today, especially with Dante Rinaldi.

Best of all was that he'd gotten to speak to Victoria again. Maybe before too long, he could invite her and her mother to Pembrook. He wanted to show them what his father had created along the banks of the Alabama River, but most of all he wanted Victoria to like it.

His only hope was that she would never discover the secret that haunted him—he would never be able to measure up to his father as the master of a large plantation.

❧

Late that afternoon Marcus pulled his horse to a stop in front of the big house at Cottonwood Plantation. He'd struggled with whether or not to ride to Dante's home ever since he'd gotten back to Pembrook from church. Finally, he had given up. He needed advice, and Dante was the only person he could ask.

He tied his horse to the hitching post at the side of the house and walked to the door. Before he had a chance to knock, a dog ran around the side of the house with Vance Rinaldi right behind. "Get back here, Jake." The boy stopped in his tracks when he spied Marcus.

Marcus smiled. "Hi, Vance. I came to see your pa. Is he home?"

Vance nodded. "Yes, sir. I'll go get him." Before Marcus could move out of the way, Vance darted in front of him, pushed the front door open, and ran inside. "Pa, there's somebody here to see you," he yelled.

"Vance, not so loud. Your father isn't deaf." Footsteps tapped on the wooden floor, and Savannah Rinaldi appeared in the house's entry. She smiled in greeting. "Marcus, it's so nice to see you again. Are you here to see Dante?"

Marcus hesitated on the porch before stepping into the house. What was he doing here? He should turn around and go home right away. When he didn't answer, Savannah directed a questioning gaze at him. Marcus swallowed and tried to smile. "I am."

She backed away from the door and motioned for him to enter. "Then come in. He's in the parlor. I'll show you the way."

He pulled the hat from his head and stepped inside the house. His gaze darted around the spacious entry and to the curving stairway that led to the second floor. "This is my first time in your home. It's beautiful."

"Thank you. I'm sorry you haven't visited us before. We must make sure you come more often in the future." Savannah glanced over her shoulder as she led the way into a room just off the hallway. "Dante," she said as they entered, "Marcus Raines is here to see you."

Dante and his daughter sat facing each other at a small game table. A chessboard rested on the tabletop between them. Dante glanced up as Savannah spoke, and a smile lit his face. "Marcus, you're just in time to save me from having to concede defeat. It's embarrassing that a nine-year-old girl can beat her father at chess." He reached over and chucked the girl under her chin. "I shouldn't have taught you so well."

The girl giggled, and Marcus stopped, unsure if he should enter. "I'm sorry. I didn't mean to disturb you."

Dante pushed up from his chair and strode forward. "It's always good to see you. Come in and have a seat. Would you like something to drink? Some tea maybe?"

Marcus shook his head. "No, I wanted to speak with you for a moment. If you're busy, I can come back later."

The girl stood and came across the room. She looped her arm through her father's. Her dark eyes lit up with a smile. "Don't worry, Mr. Raines. Our games go on forever. We'll finish later."

Dante planted a kiss on his daughter's forehead. "Thanks, Gabby. Now go see if you can find your brother. I think your mother wanted to do something with the two of you this afternoon."

"Yes, I do. Come on, Gabby." Savannah held out her hand, and her gaze drifted over her daughter before it settled on Dante. A smile pulled at the corners of her mouth, and her eyes sparkled with a silent message meant only for her husband.

Dante smiled at Savannah and hugged their daughter again before he released her. "We'll finish our game later, darling."

When Gabby and Savannah had left the room, Marcus turned to Dante. "I'm sorry to intrude."

Dante laughed and led the way to a sofa in front of the marble fireplace. "I've told you many times that you're always welcome at Cottonwood. I'm glad you finally took me up on my invitation." A large, ornate mirror with a gilt frame hung over the mantel, which held several daguerreotypes of Vance and Gabby. When Marcus had settled on the sofa, Dante eased into a chair facing him. "Now, is there a particular reason you've come this afternoon?"

The room felt stuffy, and Marcus wiped at the perspiration on his forehead with a handkerchief. "I. . .I need some help."

Dante leaned forward, a worried expression on his face. "What is it? Are you having problems at Pembrook?"

"No, nothing like that. It's. . ."

Dante frowned. "Go on. Tell me."

A large breath of air gushed from Marcus. "It's a woman."

"A woman? I don't understand." Dante's eyebrows arched.

Perspiration rolled down Marcus's cheeks. "Victoria Turner. I don't know what to do."

Understanding dawned in Dante's eyes, and he smiled. "Why, Marcus," he said, "I do believe you've come under the spell of a beautiful woman. Am I right?"

Marcus bit his lip and nodded. "Ever since I saw her get off the boat at the landing, I haven't been able to get her out of my mind. I've never had this feeling before, and it's disconcerting, to say the least."

Dante laughed. "But it's very normal. I felt the same way when I saw Savannah. I thought I would go mad from thinking about her."

Marcus scooted to the edge of the sofa. "You're the only one I felt comfortable talking to about this. That's why I've come. What do I do?"

"The question is, what do you want to do? Do you want to rid yourself of your obsession, or do you want to get to know her better?"

"I don't think I can rid my thoughts of her."

Dante laughed again. "Then you have to call on her, talk to her, see what you have in common."

Marcus stared at Dante. "Is that what you did before you married your wife?"

"No, our situation was quite different. I'll tell you about it sometime. But now I'm a father, and I'll tell you what I would want a young man to do if he was interested in my daughter."

"Good. That's what I need to know."

Dante took a deep breath. "You should go to Mr. Perkins and his sister and ask their permission to call on Victoria—that is, if the young woman wishes it. Then go to their home at night, sit in their parlor, and visit with them, get to know them, and let them see what an upstanding young man you are."

"Visit with them? Talk to them?" The thought scared

Marcus. "I don't know how to do that."

Dante leaned back in his chair and studied Marcus. "Your father kept you at home too much. You've got to learn to be more open with people. You're going to find most of them are very nice. If you're kind to them, they'll return the favor. You're going to have to make yourself likable if you ever hope to win any young woman."

Marcus raked his hand through his hair. "I know that, but it terrifies me."

Dante reached over and slapped him on the knee. "Just think of the prize. Don't be afraid. You may find that Victoria will like you as much as you do her. But there is one more thing that I would advise you to do. It made all the difference in my relationship with Savannah."

"What's that?"

"Pray about it, Marcus. You should never enter into any kind of relationship without letting God lead you."

Marcus's eyes grew wide. "Pray? I don't know how to do that."

"It's not difficult. You close your eyes and talk to God."

"That sounds too easy. You close your eyes and talk to an empty room?"

Dante leaned forward. "The room isn't empty, Marcus. You heard Daniel speak about the love that God had for us when He sent His Son to be the Savior of all mankind. Before Jesus went back to heaven, He promised that even though He would no longer be walking the earth, He would still be with us. The Bible tells us that He will never leave or forsake us."

"How is that possible?"

"When you accept Jesus as your Savior, He comes into your heart and stays there. You can feel His presence all the time."

Marcus's mouth gaped open, and he swallowed before responding. "Are you saying that I'll feel Him inside me even though I can't see Him?"

"Yes. I feel God's presence in my life all the time, and He guides me in everything I attempt. I pray over every decision I make, whether it concerns my family or the tenant farmers who live on our land. You're a shy young man, Marcus, but God can make you bold and give you strength to face whatever comes your way."

"My father never had time for God, and I suppose I haven't, either."

Dante's eyes clouded. "I spoke to your father many times about accepting Christ, but he refused. I don't want that for you. All you have to do is believe, ask Him to come into your heart, and turn your life over to Him. When I was a boy, my father taught me a Bible verse that has stayed with me: 'For God so loved the world, that he gave his only begotten Son, that whosoever believeth in him should not perish, but have everlasting life.' I hope you'll think about that verse and come to believe in the power that Jesus has to make your life right."

Marcus pondered what Dante had said before he pushed to his feet and held out his hand. "Thank you, Dante, for talking with me today. I'll think about everything you've said."

"Good." Dante stood and grasped his hand. "Don't be a stranger around here. Come again. And I wish you well with Miss Turner. Let me know how things turn out."

Marcus shrugged. "I will, but there probably won't be anything to tell. She may not even want me to call on her."

"Don't sell yourself short. You have a lot of good qualities that you try to keep hidden from people. I happen to be able to see them."

Marcus's heart pumped at the kind words. He wished his father would have said something like that to him. "Thank you, Dante. Again, I'm sorry for interrupting your Sunday afternoon at home with family."

"Nonsense. We're glad you came."

A few minutes later, Marcus mounted his horse and nudged him onto the road that led away from Cottonwood. He glanced over his shoulder at Dante and Savannah's home. The house was beautiful, but no more so than the big house at Pembrook. There was one difference that he'd noticed from the moment Savannah Rinaldi appeared in the doorway.

Cottonwood's big house was a home. Dante, Savannah, and their children loved each other. For the first time in his life, he realized what a home should be.

Pembrook had never had what he'd experienced during his short visit at Cottonwood. The only way his house would ever be a home was if love lived inside it.

He closed his eyes and envisioned walking to the front door of Pembrook and having it opened by Victoria. His blood raced through his veins at the thought. He opened his eyes, and the feeling subsided.

What was he thinking? There was no way a woman like Victoria Turner would ever be interested in him. No matter how much he longed to have a woman look at him the way Savannah had looked at Dante, he knew it wouldn't happen. His father had told him that often enough. He was destined to end up like his father—a lonely old man living in a big house with no one who loved him.

four

Victoria sat on the sofa in the small parlor of the quarters above her uncle's store. She glanced around and wondered how he'd been able to live in such cramped quarters all these years. He'd built the store five years before the war broke out and had brought his bride there to live with him until he made enough money to build a larger house. When she died two years later, he couldn't bring himself to move anywhere else. So he'd stayed on, connected to his work every hour of the day.

A stairway in the back room of the store made the upper level accessible when he was working. For after-hours visitors, a steep staircase on the back of the building led to a small landing and another entrance into the area.

When her mother first told her they would be living above the store, she had imagined the living area to be small, but she'd had no idea how little space there would be. The one good thing about their accommodations, however, was the fact that the kitchen was quite large. Her mother had been right at home in it from the moment they arrived, and the meals they'd shared around the big oak table in the middle of the room had been pleasant.

The small bedroom where she and her mother slept was quite a different story. A bed, a dresser, and an armoire they shared for storing their clothing crowded the floor space and left little room for them to navigate around each other. To make matters worse, the warm weather for the past few days had made the room quite stuffy, but the cool breeze that blew from the river through the open window had been refreshing at times.

There was no doubt about it. Victoria had no desire to spend the rest of her life living over Uncle Samuel's store.

Sighing, she directed her attention back to the book in her lap. With Uncle Samuel living alone, he'd spent much of his time reading, and his assortment of books had kept her entertained for the past few days.

This Sunday afternoon, though, she couldn't concentrate on the story she'd been reading. Her thoughts kept returning to Marcus Raines and how glad she was to see him at church. With everyone speaking to her after the sermon, she'd been delayed in leaving the building. She'd worried that he might already have left. When she saw him talking with Savannah's husband, she'd breathed a sigh of relief.

She couldn't understand why he hurried away so quickly. Most young men she knew in Mobile would have stayed longer and talked, but he seemed eager to be gone. He said he would come to the dinner after church next week, and she hoped he would. With another sigh, she picked her book up again and stared at the page where she'd stopped reading.

A knock at the outside door startled her, and she glanced up at her uncle and mother who sat in chairs facing her. Frowning, Uncle Samuel pushed to his feet. "Who could that be? I don't get many visitors on a Sunday afternoon."

Her uncle walked from the room and into the small hallway that led to the door. She listened as the door opened. "Marcus," Uncle Samuel said, "come in."

Startled at her uncle's greeting, Victoria sat up straight and tensed.

"I don't want to interrupt if you're busy." She could barely hear Marcus's words.

"Do you need something from the store?" her uncle asked.

"No, sir. I'd like to speak with you and Mrs. Turner if I may."

Victoria's heart pounded in her chest. She glanced at her mother, who directed a questioning stare at Victoria. Uncle Samuel walked into the room with Marcus right behind him. Marcus came to an abrupt stop when he saw her sitting there. She smiled, and he moved into the room.

He turned to her mother. "Good afternoon, Mrs. Turner. I hope I haven't inconvenienced you by coming unannounced."

She shook her head. "Not at all, Mr. Raines. I heard you tell my brother you wanted to talk with us." She pointed to the chair where Uncle Samuel had sat a few minutes before. "Please have a seat."

"Thank you."

Her mother turned back to her. "Victoria, perhaps you should leave us alone."

Marcus had started to sit in the chair, but he bolted upright. "No, please. I'd like for Victoria to stay."

Her mother glanced at Uncle Samuel. "Very well."

Uncle Samuel took a seat on the sofa next to Victoria. "Is something wrong, Marcus? I'm afraid I don't understand why you need to speak with us."

Marcus's blue eyes flickered over Victoria's face, and in their depths she could sense his fear. His whole demeanor suggested he might rush from the room at any moment. The muscle in his jaw twitched, and perspiration rolled down his face. He swallowed, and his Adam's apple bobbed.

"Mr. Perkins, Mrs. Turner," he began, "I'm not very good at making speeches. I don't know any way to say what I've come for than to tell you right out. I want to ask your permission to call on Victoria." His face turned crimson, and he gazed at her. "That is, if Victoria is agreeable to the idea."

Victoria's breath caught in her throat. Her eyes grew wide, and she stared at Marcus. Her uncle cleared his throat and glanced at her mother, then at her. "I appreciate the fact that you've included me in this request, but I feel like my sister and Victoria are the ones who should make the decision." He swiveled in his seat to face her. "How do you feel about what Marcus asked, Victoria?"

"It makes me very happy. I would be honored to have Marcus call on me." She stared at her mother. "Is it all right with you?"

Her mother clasped her hands in her lap and glanced at Uncle Samuel, who gave a slight shrug. "My brother tells me you're a very hardworking young man, Mr. Raines. You own one of the largest plantations in the area, but you seem to have few friends. Is this true?"

Marcus nodded. "I've lived all of my life at Pembrook, but I can assure you I'm trustworthy. And I will treat your daughter with respect."

Uncle Samuel gave an almost imperceptible nod, and her mother sank back against the cushion of the chair. "Very well, then. We give our permission for you to call on Victoria."

The smile he directed at Victoria sent ripples of pleasure floating through her body. The handsome owner of Pembrook wanted to call on her. From what she understood from Tave and Savannah, he had never shown any interest in anyone before, and now he promised her mother he would respect her.

Marcus rose from his chair and smiled at her mother. "Thank you, Mrs. Turner. I'll look forward to visiting with all of you one night this week. Tuesday, if that's all right."

"That will be fine. Victoria," her mother said, "it appears Marcus is leaving. Why don't you walk him to the door?"

His gaze followed her as she rose and brushed past him. "I'll show you out, Marcus."

She led the way to the door, opened it, and stepped back. "Thank you for coming, Marcus. You've made me very happy today."

"Have I? You may be disappointed when you get to know me better." His forehead wrinkled, and the sadness she'd seen in his eyes before returned. "I'm not like the young men you probably knew in Mobile."

She laughed. "Thank goodness for that. I'm glad you're who you are."

"I'll try not to disappoint you, Victoria." He stepped onto the landing at the top of the staircase and turned back to her. "Good day."

"Good day, Marcus. I'll expect to see you Tuesday night."

He nodded, turned, and headed down the stairs.

Victoria watched until he'd disappeared around the corner of the store before she closed the door. She stood in the hallway with her hand on the knob and thought about what had just happened.

In her wildest dreams she never would have thought a wealthy planter and owner of one of the largest plantations in the area would be interested in her. Yet he was. Marcus Raines might be shy, but he liked her. And the truth of the matter was that she liked him, too.

☙

On Tuesday night, Marcus stared at Victoria from his seat in the same chair where he'd sat on Sunday afternoon. It felt like a repeat of their previous visit, with everyone seated as if they'd been assigned specific places. Perspiration trickled down the small of his back, and he ran his finger around the inside of his shirt collar. He hadn't thought the evening that warm until he'd entered the parlor and stared into Victoria's dark eyes.

Once again he tried to determine what it was about her that fascinated him. She was beautiful, to be sure, but there was something more. Perhaps it was the lilting quality of her voice that made his heart quicken, or it could be the elegance and grace with which she moved. Whether or not he ever discovered the mystery of her hold on him, he knew he would never feel about anyone else the way he did about her. From the first moment she'd directed her sultry stare at him, he knew he was powerless to fight his attraction.

Out of the corner of his eye, he saw her mother reach toward the table beside her where a tray with a tea service rested. She glanced at his empty cup. "More tea?"

He shook his head and handed her the cup and saucer he'd drained within seconds of its being offered. "No thank you. That was delicious."

Her mother collected the other cups and stood. "I'll take the tray into the kitchen if everyone is finished."

Marcus jumped to his feet. "Allow me to carry it for you."

She shook her head. "There's no need for that. Samuel can help me."

Mr. Perkins stood up, his eyes wide. "Of course."

As they disappeared out the door, Marcus glanced at Victoria and swallowed the panic that roiled in his stomach. "I—it's good to see you again, Miss Turner."

She frowned and picked up a fan that lay beside her in the chair. She snapped the ribbing of the fan open in front of her face and peered over its semicircular top. Her dark eyes bored into his. "I thought we'd agreed to call each other by our first names."

His throat constricted. "W—we d—did. I'm sorry, Victoria."

She lowered the fan and smiled. "That's better, Marcus." She inclined her head in the direction of the kitchen. "You know they went to the kitchen so that we could visit without them in the room."

He darted a glance toward the door and back to her. "I didn't think about them leaving us alone."

Victoria tilted her head to one side and smiled. "You are so serious and so formal. How am I ever going to get you to relax and just talk with me?"

He exhaled. "I haven't had much practice talking with a woman."

"Are you scared of women, Marcus?"

"I've never given it much thought. I don't know that many women."

She studied him for a moment. "Then maybe you're afraid of me."

His gaze drifted over her face, and in that moment he knew she wasn't the one who scared him. He shook his head. "It's not you. It's myself that I fear the most."

Her eyes grew wide. "But why?"

"I grew up at Pembrook with my father. The only women around were the wives of the tenant farmers, and I didn't know any of them well. So sitting here talking with you is a new experience for me. I want to do everything I can to impress you and make you like me, but I'm afraid I'll fail."

"And what makes you think that?"

He scooted to the edge of his chair and clasped his hands between his knees. "Even though I've lived at Pembrook all my life, I feel like an outsider in the community. Dante

Rinaldi is the only man who's ever talked to me—besides the preacher, that is. Every time I see him, he invites me to church. I think he was shocked I came last Sunday."

"I'm glad you came, too. But it doesn't matter what other people think about you. I make up my mind about my friends based on how I feel. I like you, Marcus."

"You do now, but if you change your mind, I'll understand. You see, we've had very different lives. You've lost your father, but you have a wonderful mother. I can tell how much love there is between the two of you by the way you look at each other. I never knew my mother. My father met and married her when he visited Boston and brought her back to Pembrook. She hated life in Alabama almost as much as she disliked being a mother. She deserted us right before the war and returned to her family. I never heard from her again."

A small frown pulled at her eyebrows. "I'm so sorry. That must have been very hard for you."

"It was. My father saw that I had the best tutors, but they were paid to be nice to me. They really didn't care about me. No one has ever asked me to be their friend until you did. The truth is, I don't know much about friendships or how to talk with people. Especially with a beautiful young woman."

Her mouth curled into a smile. "Do you think I'm beautiful, Marcus?"

He couldn't tear his gaze away from her lips. "You're the most beautiful woman I've ever seen. You're young and full of life, not at all like me. I've inherited a plantation that I'm trying to run like my father did, and I spend all my time thinking about cotton and corn crops. You must have had interesting friends in Mobile."

"I did have a lot of friends. Two of them, Margaret and Clara, were more like sisters. Not only did we attend church together, but we also lived on the same street. I didn't want to leave them."

Marcus hesitated before he asked the question that had been on his mind for days. "Was there also a special gentleman friend you didn't want to leave?"

A smile pulled at her lips. "No, Marcus. There was no man in my life."

Her words made his heart beat faster. "I hope living in Willow Bend won't be too much of a disappointment for you. I'm sure you'll make all kinds of friends soon."

"All the way up the river I tried to think of some way I could get back to Mobile. Then I saw something that excited me."

"What was it?"

"Pembrook. It took my breath away when I spied that beautiful house on the bluff. I wondered about the people who lived there. Then we arrived in Willow Bend, and you were on the dock. It was almost like you were waiting for me to arrive. I knew right away we were going to be great friends."

Her long lashes fell over the dark eyes that stirred his heart, and he leaned back in his chair. She was right. Without knowing it, he had been waiting for her to arrive and had been for years. Now that he had found her, he wasn't going to give her up.

five

On Sunday when the final *Amen* was said, Marcus waited at the back pew in hopes of speaking with Victoria as she left the church. Tom Jackson nodded as he and his wife passed by. "Good to see you today, Marcus."

"Thank you," he mumbled and directed his attention back to Victoria walking up the aisle toward him.

She smiled at him as she approached and stopped beside him. "I'm glad you're here, Marcus."

Several women clustered together in a pew near the front of the sanctuary. They held their fans in front of their mouths as they talked, but they didn't take their eyes off him. He felt sure he was the topic of conversation with many of the churchgoers today.

"My presence seems to have stirred quite a bit of interest today."

"I'm sure everyone's happy you're here." She glanced to the foyer where the pastor and his wife stood. "Let's go speak to the Lucketts; then you can walk me out to the picnic grove where the ladies are getting the food ready."

Reverend Luckett's face broke into a smile when they approached. "Marcus, I can't tell you how pleased I am. You've been here two Sundays in a row." His eyes twinkled as he glanced at Victoria. "If you'd moved to Willow Bend a long time ago, Marcus might already be a member of our church."

Victoria laughed and gazed up at him. "We'll have to work

on him harder now, I suppose."

She cast a glance at him, and he followed her out the church and down the front steps. When they reached the bottom, he stopped. "Were you serious about our walking together to the picnic area?"

With a sigh, she opened the white lace parasol in her hand and raised it to shade her face. "Marcus Raines, for a man who runs a large plantation, you act like a scared schoolboy. In the last week you've been to my home three times counting your visit last Sunday. I think that makes it official that you're calling on me. Now don't you think the next step is to let the good people of Willow Bend in on the news?"

He couldn't help laughing. His heart felt lighter than it had in years. "Oh, Victoria," he said, "you're the most delightful woman I've ever known."

She held her hand at her waist and gave a quick curtsy. "Thank you, kind sir. And may I say that you're the most fascinating man I've ever known."

He could hardly believe what she'd said. He threw his shoulders back and puffed out his chest. "Then let's go see what the good ladies have fixed for us to eat today."

They walked toward the tables that had been set up under the trees in the church yard. He spotted Dante Rinaldi sitting on the ground, surrounded by a group of children. He handed a kite to his son, Vance, and the boys jumped up and ran off. Dante stood and joined one of the groups of men scattered across the yard. With the exception of his encounters with Dante, Marcus had had very few conversations with any of the men. Imbeciles, his father had called most of the planters in the area—except Dante. There was a quality in the man that demanded respect, and even his father had recognized that.

Marcus glanced at the woman beside him. He didn't want to think about his father today or the mother he'd never known. He wanted to concentrate on Victoria and the hold she already had on his heart. She was like a breath of fresh air that had entered his life, and he wanted to enjoy every minute he was with her.

&

"I see Dante and Marcus have settled under that tree where I spread out some quilts. Let's go join them." Savannah didn't wait for Victoria to answer but led the way toward where the men sat.

Victoria's skirts skimmed the surface of the grass as she followed Savannah to the spot. She had waited with her food until Savannah had finished helping serve all the children, who were the last to line up at the tables. Now she looked forward to getting to know the woman who had welcomed her into the community.

The men jumped to their feet as Savannah and Victoria approached. Dante took his wife's plate and waited for her to sit and settle her skirts before he handed the food to her. Victoria tried to hide her amused smile as Marcus studied Dante's movements before he turned to her and took her plate in his hands.

When she was seated on the ground, Marcus dropped down beside her and handed her the food. He'd taken off the black coat he'd worn to church and rolled up the sleeves of his white shirt.

Even when she'd met him on the docks, she'd detected a formality in his manner, and she had seen it during his visits to see her. Today he appeared more relaxed. He seemed to really be enjoying himself, and it made her happy.

Dante shoveled another forkful of potatoes in his mouth, chewed, and swallowed. "This is mighty fine eating. We ought to have dinner every Sunday after church."

Savannah chuckled and raised her eyebrows. "You wouldn't think so if you had to cook."

He leaned closer to his wife and patted her hand. "Why would I want to when I have the best cook in the county living in my house?"

Savannah sniffed and sat up straighter. "Mamie doesn't live in our house."

Dante threw back his head and roared with laughter. "No, she doesn't. I was talking about you, but I forgot who taught you how to cook."

Victoria smiled at the exchange between the two and turned to Savannah. "Who is Mamie?"

"She and her husband were slaves at Cottonwood," Savannah said. "Even after they were freed and my parents had died, they wouldn't leave me. When Dante bought Cottonwood, Mamie's husband, Saul, became the first tenant farmer. Mamie has been my second mother all my life, and now she's getting older. But she can still cook better than anyone else in the county."

Dante nodded. "She sure can. I'm fortunate that Savannah learned from her." He leaned closer and whispered in a loud voice to Marcus. "Sometimes I slip off to Saul and Mamie's house just so I can sit down and eat with them."

Savannah laughed and glanced at Victoria. "He thinks it's a secret, but I've always known it."

Victoria turned to Marcus, who'd sat wide-eyed through the exchange between the couple. "Who cooks for you at Pembrook?"

Surprise flashed on his face, and he glanced around at

those who stared at him. "S–Sally M–Moses," he stammered.

Dante nodded. "Oh, I know who that is. She's the wife of Ben Moses. Her son, James, is a friend of Henry Walton, who lives at Cottonwood."

Marcus frowned. "I've never understood how they can be friends. Henry's white, and James. . ."

"Isn't," Dante finished for him. "At Cottonwood we look at each other as equals. The color of a person's skin doesn't matter to us. We work together to make all our lives better."

"I see," Marcus said and directed his attention back to his plate.

"Uh-oh," Dante moaned and jumped to his feet. "Savannah, it looks like our son is engaged in battle again. We'd better go break up his fight before somebody gets hurt."

Savannah jumped to her feet and hurried toward a group of boys who minutes before had been playing together. Now Vance and another boy rolled and tumbled on the ground.

Victoria laughed. "Poor Vance. I think he's in for it now."

"I think you're right." Marcus chuckled.

They watched as Savannah and Dante pulled Vance off the boy and marched him toward the church. When they'd disappeared around the back of the building, Victoria leaned forward. "Are you having a good time, Marcus?"

He shrugged. "I guess."

The answer made her gasp. She had expected him to say that spending time with her was always fun, but he hadn't. "Aren't you happy to be with me today?"

He set his plate down and nodded. "Of course I am. I was just thinking about what Dante said about the tenant farmers at Pembrook. He acts like they're almost family. I've never known anyone who felt that way."

Victoria waved her hand in dismissal. "Don't think about

things like tenant farmers and crops today. I want us to have some fun. You're always so serious. I want to hear you laugh and tell me what a good time you're having."

"I always have a good time with you, Victoria."

"Then you might show it by relaxing a little."

He smiled. "I thought I was relaxed."

She tilted her head and studied him. "No, I think your problem is that you don't laugh enough."

"I'm a serious person, but I do laugh when something's funny." He pushed his plate aside. "I'll give you a challenge. Make me laugh."

She chewed on her lip for a moment before her mouth pulled into a grin. "I could tell you about some of my adventures when I was a child, but you might decide not to call on me anymore."

"Were you a mischievous little girl?" He cocked an eyebrow at her.

"Oh, worse than that." She looked over her shoulder, leaned toward him, and whispered, "I was horrid."

A tiny smile pulled at his lips. "I can't believe that."

"Oh, but I was. For instance, one time my mother sent me out to gather the eggs from the henhouse. I started back inside with a basketful, but for some unknown reason I walked behind the henhouse, took an egg from the basket, and threw it against the back of the building. I watched the yolk and the whites of the egg trickle down the wood, and it amazed me how slowly they moved. So I threw another one to see if its contents would move faster. Then another and another until every egg in the basket lay broken on the ground."

He chuckled. "I'll bet your mother didn't like that."

"No, she didn't. But she wasn't as upset as she was the time

I threw a broken plate at her best friend's son, who was five years older than me."

Marcus's eyes grew wide. "Was he hurt?"

Victoria grinned. "I thought he looked good with a two-inch gash over his eyebrow."

A soft laugh rumbled in Marcus's throat.

"But I suppose the worst thing I ever did happened when my parents and I visited Uncle Samuel when I was about six years old. I was bored and wanted to go home. I'd been whining all day, and my mother was about to lose her patience. Finally, I told her if they weren't going to take me to Mobile, I would go on my own. She told me she was going to spank me if I didn't quit nagging. I went in the bedroom, crawled under the bed, and hid."

"What happened?"

"They missed me and started looking. I heard them calling, but I didn't say a word. After they checked the bedroom and didn't see me, they went back to the store to look for me. I fell asleep. When they couldn't find me, my mother became upset. She was afraid I'd run away. Then she began to think things like I'd fallen in the river and drowned. The whole town turned out to look for me. When I woke up and crawled out from under that bed, they were so glad to see me. That is, until they realized I'd been hiding."

"And?"

"And my father gave me the worst spanking of my life. I never pulled that trick again."

Marcus threw back his head and laughed. "Oh, Victoria. You are the most interesting woman I've ever known. I don't think anyone's made me feel this good in my whole life."

Victoria watched him for a moment before she spoke. "Maybe it's good I've told you these things, Marcus. My mother has always told me I'm too impulsive. I do things and think about the consequences later. You may not like that in a woman."

His hand inched across the quilt, and she slid hers toward it until their fingertips touched. "I like everything about you. Don't ever change. You make me happy."

She glanced across the yard and saw Savannah and Dante returning. She jerked her hand away, picked up her plate, and took a bite. He did the same, but Victoria noticed that he smiled as he ate. She hoped what he said about her making him happy was true, because she'd been happier since she met Marcus than she could ever remember. She could hardly wait to see where their relationship would take them.

❧

An hour later with all the food eaten and the dishes cleared away, the congregation drifted into groups across the picnic grove to spend an afternoon visiting. Marcus and Dante had left the tree where they'd been sitting while Victoria and Savannah helped clear the tables. She caught sight of Marcus standing next to Dante in a group of men beside the church. At times a loud voice would erupt from within the circle, but she couldn't make out what was being said.

Seated on a quilt again, Victoria placed her arms behind her, flattened her palms, and leaned back. "What do you suppose those men are talking about?"

Savannah chuckled and smoothed her skirts. "The main topic of conversation around here is the weather. Our crops depend on whether we get too much or not enough rain. We can't control it, so we talk about it."

Victoria studied Marcus, who appeared to be taking in everything that was being said. She didn't see him participate in the exchange, and she wondered why. She smiled at

Savannah. "Life in a farming community is so new to me. It may take me some time to get used to it, but today has been a great start. I can't thank you and Tave enough for planning this outing so I could meet everyone."

Savannah stared past Victoria's shoulder. "Speaking of Tave, here she comes now." Savannah patted the empty spot on the quilt beside her. "Come and join us."

Tave dropped onto the quilt and sighed. "I don't mind if I do. Martha Thompson caught me just as I was about to come over here. I thought I'd never get away from her."

Victoria narrowed her eyes and stared at the women seated in chairs near the tables where the food had been earlier. She tried to remember which one was Martha, but it was no use. Remembering all of their names had proven to be a bigger task than she thought.

Victoria frowned and turned back to Tave. "Is something wrong with Martha that makes you dislike her?"

Savannah grinned and leaned closer to Victoria. "Now don't misunderstand. We love Martha. She is always the first to be there when someone is in need. But sometimes it seems like she may have an ulterior motive."

"What?" Victoria asked.

Tave sighed. "She wants to be the first one to get all the facts about everyone's personal business."

"Oh," Victoria said, "she's the town gossip. Did she want you to tell her something today? Is that why you couldn't get away from her?"

Tave nodded. "I'm afraid she didn't want to know anything different than what every other woman here today is dying to find out."

"And what's that?"

Tave glanced at Savannah. "What in the world have you

done to get Marcus Raines interested in you?"

The question stunned Victoria, and she stared at her two new friends. "I have no idea what you're talking about."

Savannah arched her eyebrows. "Come now, Victoria. Marcus is almost a recluse out at Pembrook. His whole life revolves around that plantation. He hardly ever comes to town, and when he does, he completes his business and hurries home. He doesn't accept invitations, and he doesn't extend any. All of a sudden, you show up in Willow Bend, and Marcus is a different person."

"How is he different?"

Tave scooted closer to her. "Daniel has been the pastor at the church for nearly three years now. He's prayed for Marcus ever since he's known him and invited him to church every time he's seen him, but he never would come. You arrive, and he's attended for the last two Sundays."

"Not only that," Savannah added, "but he came to Cottonwood last Sunday to talk to Dante. He wanted to know what he should do to get to know you better. Dante advised him to speak with your mother and uncle and ask their permission to call on you. Did he do that?"

"Yes," Victoria murmured.

"How many times has he been to see you?"

"Three."

Stunned expressions covered the faces of both women. "Three?" Tave said. "I've never heard of him going to see anybody once, and you say he's been to visit you three times."

Victoria's face warmed, and she directed her gaze to the quilt. She ran her hand over one of the squares that made up the quilt top. "He's only been to see me twice, but I counted last Sunday when he came to ask permission to call on me."

Savannah laughed. "He must have gone straight there

after leaving Cottonwood." She leaned forward and patted Victoria's hand. "I would say you have yourself a serious suitor."

Tave's eyes narrowed. "And what do you think about that, Victoria?"

She squirmed under the intense scrutiny of Tave's eyes. "I. . .I really don't know. I suppose I feel honored that a man who owns a large plantation would be interested in me. I don't have any money, and I'm not sophisticated. I have no idea why he'd like me."

Tave glanced at the men across the yard and back to Victoria. "Be careful. No one knows Marcus well. I don't want to see you hurt."

Victoria laughed. "I won't be."

"There's something else that concerns us, Victoria." Savannah glanced at Tave and took a deep breath. "Marcus isn't a believer. That may seem like a small thing right now, but it can cause big problems if your friendship with Marcus gets stronger."

"He's been to church for the last two Sundays. That should show you that he's not a bad person."

Tave sighed. "I'm not saying he's a bad person, but he's told Daniel several times that he has no need for God in his life. The Bible warns Christians not to become yoked to unbelievers. You really need to be careful. Hasn't your mother ever discussed this with you?"

Victoria shook her head. "No. My father often spoke to me about choosing friends who were believers, but my mother has always been concerned that I would marry a man who could provide for me." She smiled. "Besides, Marcus is a friend. It's not like he's asked me to marry him."

Savannah narrowed her eyes and leaned forward. "You can

never tell where a friendship will lead. Be careful, Victoria. I wouldn't want to see you get hurt."

Victoria sighed. Marcus was handsome, and he was rich. And he was attending church with her. What more could she want?

She was sure, however, that her new friends only had her best interests in mind. Both women possessed a gentle quality that made her feel as if she'd known them forever, and they seemed genuinely concerned about her relationship with Marcus.

She glanced over at the group where Marcus still stood. As if he felt her eyes on him, he turned and stared at her. A smile creased his mouth, and her heart pumped. In that moment, she knew it made no difference what her new friends said.

Since the moment she'd seen him on the dock, he'd been in her mind, and he said he'd thought about her. If that was true, she had been offered an opportunity like she never would have imagined. All she had to do to escape her lifetime sentence as a clerk in a general store and become the mistress of a great plantation was to make Marcus Raines fall in love with her. Something told her that wouldn't be too difficult.

six

Marcus tried to concentrate on the conversation of the men around him, but all he could think about was Victoria seated underneath a tree across the picnic grounds. He glanced at her every chance he got so that he could memorize what she looked like today. It would give him something to think about as he drifted off to sleep tonight.

With a sinking heart, he realized the conversation around him had halted and that all the men stared at him as if they waited for him to speak. He had no idea what had been said during the last few minutes or what was expected of him.

He darted a pleading glance at Dante. "I'm sorry. What did you say?"

Dante's mouth twisted into a grin. "We were discussing our crops. How many acres would you say your tenant farmers will plant this spring?"

Marcus swallowed back the panic that had risen in his throat and cast a grateful smile in Dante's direction. "Altogether I think we'll probably have about a thousand acres in cotton and corn. We'll leave the rest of the acreage for livestock forage."

Dante nodded. "Last summer was so hot the fescue didn't do well in the pastures. Maybe this year will be better."

The men mumbled their agreement. Dante opened his mouth to say something else but stopped when his son ran up beside him. "What is it, Vance?"

Vance closed one eye, tilted his head to the side, and stared up at his father. "Mama says it's time for us to be going home."

Dante patted the boy on the head and laughed. "Go tell her I'll be right there."

"Yes, sir." The boy scampered back toward his mother.

Dante watched until Vance stopped beside Savannah before he addressed the group again. "I suppose I'd better get going." He shook hands with each man. "Have a safe week, and I hope to see all of you next Sunday."

Marcus turned to look back at Victoria, but she was no longer sitting under the tree. She walked toward the church beside Savannah, who held Vance's hand. He fell into step beside Dante. "I'll walk back with you."

As they ambled across the picnic grounds, Dante pulled a watch from his pocket. "It's later than I thought. I was having such a good time I forgot all about the chores waiting at home. Livestock don't take Sundays off. They expect to be fed on schedule."

The words surprised Marcus. "You don't feed your own livestock, do you?"

Dante laughed. "Of course I do. Who else would?"

"Your tenant farmers. They feed mine."

Dante frowned. "Even on Sundays?"

"Yes. Why should Sunday be any different?"

Dante stopped and faced Marcus. "At Cottonwood, I like for my tenant farmers to have Sundays with their families. They have chores at their homes that have to be done, and I don't want to take up their time doing mine, too. Everybody works hard all week, including the women and children. I believe they deserve some time to be together and enjoy the day."

Marcus stared at Dante in amazement. "But you have so many cows, not to mention the hogs and horses. How do you feed all of them by yourself?"

"During the week, some boys whose fathers are tenant farmers do the feeding for me. On Sundays, Savannah, Gabby, and Vance help me."

Marcus's mouth gaped open. "You make your family work?"

Dante laughed. "You make it sound like it's something horrible. There's nothing wrong with honest work, Marcus. Savannah and I have struggled to bring Cottonwood back, and we want Gabby and Vance to understand the value of hard work and to appreciate the people who help to make their life more comfortable."

"You make it sound like the tenant farmers are your equals. Surely you don't believe that."

"Oh, but I do, Marcus. The Bible tells us that we're all God's children. No one is more important than another. I want my children to understand that."

Marcus shook his head. "You certainly have some strange ideas, Dante."

Sadness flickered in Dante's eyes. "I tried to talk to your father many times about my beliefs, but he always dismissed me. I hope you'll be more open to what God teaches about loving each other."

He glanced at Victoria's retreating figure and smiled. "I'm certainly open to love."

Dante followed his gaze and turned to frown at him. "I'm not talking about the romantic love a man feels for a woman. I'm talking about the kind of love that is voluntary and unconditional. It allows a person to look at his enemy and love him because God does."

"That sounds impossible. I couldn't love an enemy."

"Maybe you have to start closer to home, Marcus. I've heard rumors that some of your tenant farmers are looking for somewhere else to go next spring. They say living at Pembrook is a lot like slavery."

Marcus's heart pounded from the temper that flared inside him. "So they're looking for somewhere else. Who are they? Tell me, and I'll take care of them."

Dante shook his head. "I don't know any names, and I wouldn't tell you if I did. I've only told you this because I know how difficult it will be to farm your land if you lose tenants. Think about how you treat the people who work with you, and try to make them feel like they're an important part of your success. In reality, they are."

Marcus straightened to his full height. "They'd better realize how good they have it at Pembrook."

Dante put his hand on Marcus's shoulder. "I don't want you to be angry. My only reason for talking like this to you is to help you. Please believe me. I know it hasn't been easy since your father died. You have big responsibilities that require great strength of character. I want you to be successful."

No one had ever spoken to him in such a forthright way before. Yet Dante's words were tempered with compassion. A few days ago, Marcus had told Victoria he'd never had a friend in Willow Bend. He realized now that wasn't true. Dante Rinaldi had been there all the time, but he hadn't recognized the friendship he offered.

Marcus swallowed and nodded. "Thank you for speaking so frankly with me. I'll think about what you said."

Dante smiled. "Good. Now why don't we catch up with the ladies? I'm sure Victoria would like to say good-bye to you before you leave."

Marcus followed Dante as he headed toward where his wife and Victoria had stopped. When they reached the two women, Savannah smiled at her husband. "I have everything in the buggy. If you'll hold on to Vance, I'll see if I can find Gabby."

Dante cocked an eyebrow and grabbed the boy's hand. "You heard your mother. Let's go wait in the buggy." He turned to Victoria. "Let me welcome you to Willow Bend again and tell you how glad we are you've come to live in our town."

She reached out and grasped Savannah's hand. "Thank you for planning this wonderful gathering. I feel much more at home now that I'm getting to know folks."

Savannah squeezed her hand. "Good. I'll try to get into town this week and stop by the store."

Dante rolled his eyes and grinned. "She'll be there Wednesday afternoon, Victoria. I believe that's the day the *Montgomery Belle* is expected on its trip back downriver. Savannah will make sure she gets to see the boat."

Vance put his hand over his mouth and snickered, but Savannah only squared her shoulders and sniffed. "I'm going to find Gabby," she said and disappeared around the side of the church.

Marcus watched Dante head toward the buggy with his son before he glanced back at Victoria. "They're quite a couple, aren't they?"

Victoria smiled. "Yes, they are." She shaded her eyes with her hand and stared toward the picnic area. "Now where did Mama go?" she murmured.

A slight frown pulled at her eyebrows, and her mouth opened just enough to expose her white teeth. He couldn't take his eyes off her. She had to be the most beautiful woman he'd ever seen.

His eyes grew wide. What was wrong with him? His father

had warned him that women would beguile a man and make him believe they offered love. All they ever wanted, he had said, was a man's money. If that's what Victoria wanted, maybe he should stay away from her for a while, just until he had rid himself of the spell she had cast on him. He cleared his throat. "Victoria."

She lowered her eyelids and smiled. "Yes, Marcus."

"I know I came to call on you last Tuesday and Friday nights, but I don't think that's going to be possible this week."

The lips that made his heart race drooped into a pout. "Don't you want to see me, Marcus?"

His heart pricked at the sight of moisture in her eyes. Was it possible that his words had hurt her to the point of making her cry? He felt as if her tears had seeped through his pores and flooded through his body. He was drowning in the need to be with her, and there was nothing he could do about it.

He took a deep breath. "Of course I want to see you. I wondered if your mother would mind if I came three nights this week."

Victoria smiled, and she inched closer to him. His heart soared. "My mother wouldn't mind, and it would make me very happy. In fact, I'd like it if you came every night."

At that moment, her mother and uncle stopped beside them. "It's time to go, Victoria," her mother said. She turned to Marcus. "We hope to see you again soon."

He glanced down at Victoria and smiled. "I'll probably come to visit tomorrow night if that's all right."

Victoria flashed him a big smile. "That sounds wonderful. We'll see you then."

He didn't mount his horse until Mr. Perkins's buggy had pulled away from the church. Then he climbed on and turned the mare toward Pembrook. It had been an unsettling day. The problems at Pembrook that Dante had warned him of were troubling enough, but he also found himself beginning a relationship with a woman he'd only known for a week. He had no idea how to address either matter.

ቈ

Two months later on a Sunday afternoon, Victoria sat in a chair underneath a tree in back of her uncle's store. She'd hoped the shade would provide some relief from the heat that stifled her in the upstairs living quarters, but it hadn't. If it was this hot in the middle of June, she dreaded what July and August would bring.

There wasn't a leaf stirring on any of the trees today. The still air pressed down on her like a great weight. She closed her eyes and listened—for a bird's call, the laughter of children playing up and down the main street, the nicker of horse—but she heard nothing in the quiet afternoon.

She swished her hand fan in front of her face and let her mind drift to the church service earlier today. Over the weeks, she'd learned the names of all the families in the congregation and which pew they sat in each Sunday. Uncle Samuel liked to be about halfway back, and she could spot where they would sit the minute she walked in the door. She doubted if it took Reverend Luckett but a few minutes to make a mental note of who was absent from the service.

A smile pulled at her lips as she thought of Marcus, who had sat beside her for the past month at church. It had taken him a few weeks to get up the nerve to ask if he could join them, and she had been thrilled. His presence beside her made her pulse race, but she tried not to let her facial expression show what was happening inside her.

This morning as they shared a hymnal, his finger had

accidentally brushed hers on the back of the book. He gasped and glanced at her as if begging her pardon. She smiled at him, slid her hand across the back of the book, and stroked his knuckle. It was a brazen gesture, and her mother would have fainted if she'd seen it. The reward of his blue eyes sparkling at her had made her overture worth it.

"Good afternoon."

Her eyes flew open at the sound of Marcus's voice, and she jerked up straight in her chair. The book in her lap tumbled to the ground, and Marcus knelt in front of her and scooped it up. He smiled as he handed it back to her.

"Marcus, you scared me. I didn't hear your horse. Where is it?"

"I tied my mare to the hitching post out front and walked around here."

She reached up and smoothed her hair back into the bun at the nape of her neck. "I wasn't expecting you this afternoon."

He glanced around. "And I didn't expect to find you alone without your mother or uncle around."

"They decided to take a nap, but I couldn't sleep. It's so hot upstairs, and there are only a few windows. Every once in a while we get a breeze off the river, but not often."

He dropped down on the ground beside her and stared at the back of her uncle's store. "I'm glad my grandfather put a lot of windows in the big house. It helps a lot in the summertime."

"That sounds nice. The summers in Mobile are hot, too, but our house had a small garden with some large shade trees. I spent a lot of time outside."

He stared at her for a moment. "You must miss Mobile a lot."

She shook her head. "I would have missed it more if I hadn't met you."

He directed his gaze to a sprig of grass and pulled at it. "I just happened to be there when you arrived. Now that you feel more comfortable in Willow Bend, I'm sure there are a lot of young men who would like to get to know you better."

A retort that she had no wish to see other men hovered on her tongue, but she bit it back. Marcus had been calling on her for the last two months, and his actions told her he liked her. She didn't know why he couldn't say the words. Was this going to be their relationship forever? They'd sit in her parlor with her mother and uncle in the next room while he talked about his crops and what he planned to do at Pembrook?

If that was all he wanted, she might do well to move on. The thought made her sad. Marcus had come to mean a lot to her, but she had no idea how he felt about her. He had sought out her company and had called on her at least twice a week and sometimes more, but he never spoke of personal feelings. Maybe he never would.

She had to do something with her life. If her relationship with Marcus was going to lead nowhere, perhaps she needed to follow through on her threat to return to Mobile. If Uncle Samuel would loan her enough money for passage and living expenses for a few months, she felt sure she could stay at the boardinghouse where she'd worked. Maybe her old job would be available. If not, she'd look for other employment. That's what she would do—she would return to Mobile and put all thoughts of Marcus Raines out of her mind.

She sighed. "If there are any young men who want to get to know me, they'd better hurry."

He tilted his head to one side and frowned up at her. "Why?"

Her hands trembled. She flattened them on her skirt and smoothed out the fabric. "Because I probably won't be here much longer."

His eyes grew wide, and his mouth dropped open. "Why? Are you going somewhere?"

She nodded. "I told my mother when we came here I didn't expect to stay long. I think it's about time for me to go back to Mobile."

He jumped to his feet. "I had no idea you were thinking of leaving."

She stood and faced him. "I've been thinking about it ever since we got here. I can't see anything here for me except ending up as an unmarried woman who's spent her whole life working in a general store and living above it. I want more than that."

"And you don't think you can find what you want here?"

She let her gaze wander over his face. "Not if it means living above a store."

"Victoria," he said, "I don't want you to leave. I would miss you."

She eased toward him. She opened her mouth and touched the tip of her tongue to her upper lip. "I'll miss you, too, Marcus. I think about you all the time."

He couldn't take his eyes off her lips. The longer he stared, the redder his face became. After a moment, he shook his head and backed away. "I have to go. I'll come back one night this week. Please consider your choices carefully before you make a final decision."

"I will."

He turned and strode around the side of the store. Victoria stood still until she heard his horse gallop away. Then she dropped down in her chair.

What had she done? As she thought back to what she'd said, her face burned. Her words sounded like she dared Marcus to do something to make her stay. Her mother had often warned her she was too impulsive, and she certainly had been today. If Marcus thought she was pressing him for a commitment, she'd probably never see him again. She had just scared off the one man who had ever shown any attention to her. All she could do now was follow through on her threat and begin making preparations to leave for Mobile.

The thought of being away from Marcus crushed her heart, and tears filled her eyes. She sank down in the chair and covered her face with her hands. What had she done?

❧

Marcus dug his heels into the horse's side and galloped out of Willow Bend along the river toward Pembrook. He couldn't believe it. Victoria was going to return to Mobile.

There had to be something he could do to keep her here. For the first time in his life, he'd met someone who made him glad to be alive, and he didn't want to lose her. He gritted his teeth and groaned. If he'd never gone to see her that first time, he wouldn't be so unhappy now. He should have kept his distance and not discovered how her very presence made his pulse race. But he had chosen to go. Now he was going to pay for that choice.

If only he knew what to do. She said she didn't want to end up an unmarried woman still working in a store. He didn't know why she should worry. As beautiful as she was, some man would be happy to make her his wife. Anger roiled in his stomach at the thought of Victoria with another man.

What was it she had said? That when she arrived at

Willow Bend it was as if he was waiting for her. He'd had the same thought many times.

He pulled back on the reins, and the horse stopped in the road. Marcus leaned on the saddle's pommel and frowned. She'd said she wanted more out of life than what she had at her uncle's home. But what if he could give her more? Maybe it had been decided the day something made him go to the riverboat landing to wait for his cotton planters. He'd had no idea he would encounter a beautiful woman, but he had. Was there some way he could control her decision about leaving?

His mouth pulled into a smile at the answer that came to mind. Of course he could. He knew exactly what to do. Turning the horse around, he spurred the mare toward town.

Within minutes he was back at the store. He jumped out of the saddle before the horse had come to a complete stop. He looped the reins over the hitching post, clenched his fists, and strode toward the back of the store where he'd left Victoria.

She still sat in the chair, but her hands covered her face and her shoulders shook. Shocked at the sight of her crying, he slowed his step and crept toward her. When he stood in front of her, he knelt on one knee. "Victoria, what's the matter?"

She jerked her head up and stared at him with a startled expression on her face. "What do you want?"

He felt at a loss as to what he should do. "I came back to apologize for leaving so abruptly."

She pushed up out of the chair and stepped behind it. "There's no need for that. I'm all right."

He frowned. "No, you're not. Did I do something to offend you?"

She shook her head. "You didn't do anything."

He wanted to step closer to her, but the chair blocked his way. "I came back to tell you that you're not going back to Mobile."

Her eyebrows arched. "I'm not?"

"No, you're going to stay here and marry me." He could hardly believe he'd spoken the words.

Her hand clutched at her throat, and she stared at him. "You want me to marry you?"

He reached out, grabbed the chair, and set it to the side. Then he stepped closer to her. "I would regret it the rest of my life if I didn't stop you from leaving. You don't want to end up living over a store. I have a beautiful home that needs a woman in it. I want you to marry me and live with me at Pembrook."

Fresh tears welled up in her eyes. "What about love, Marcus? Do you love me?"

He hesitated before he answered. "I haven't had any experience with love, Victoria. All I know is that you are in my thoughts constantly and that I feel more at ease with you than anyone I've ever known. I can't imagine my life without you. I'm a wealthy man, and I want to provide you with everything you need in life. When I think of all those things, I know I love you with all my heart."

"You've been in my thoughts since I first met you, too. I don't want to go back to Mobile. I love you, too, Marcus. I want to stay here and be your wife."

Her words stirred his heart. "My wife," he murmured. He'd never dreamed he would be able to say those words, and she'd also said she loved him. He reached out, took her hand in his, and kissed it. "Thank you, Victoria. You do me a great honor. Now that we've settled our wishes, I must ask your family's permission."

"Do you want to talk to them now?"

He shook his head. "No. I'll invite all of you to Pembrook after church next Sunday. I want them to see where you'll be living and be assured you'll be cared for. Then I'll speak with them. This moment has meant so much to me, and I wish it to remain between the two of us until then. Is that agreeable with you?"

"Yes, that's fine with me."

He took a deep breath. "There is one more thing, Victoria."

"What?"

He grasped both her hands in his and stared into her eyes. "You must promise you will never leave me."

Her eyes narrowed. "Why do you think I'd leave you?"

He rubbed his fingers across her knuckles. "My mother left me when I was small, and I've never had a woman in my life until you."

She didn't blink as she returned his steady gaze. "I promise I will never leave you, Marcus."

He exhaled, dropped her hands, and backed away. "Good. I shall be back tomorrow night to invite your family to Pembrook."

He turned and hurried back to where he'd left his horse. At the corner of the store, he glanced over his shoulder at her. She raised her hand and waved. He pursed his lips and nodded before he continued on his way.

When he'd awoken this morning, he'd had no idea he would be engaged before the end of the day. His father's words about how a woman couldn't be trusted flashed into his mind. Father had felt that way because of his wife's desertion. She had deserted not only her husband but her son as well.

For the first time in a long time, Marcus allowed the

emotions he normally struggled to conceal to flow through his mind. He tried again to remember what his mother had looked like, but with his father's refusal to have her picture in the house, he had no idea. He allowed the vision he'd stored away in the hollow part of his heart to drift to the surface, and he smiled. Did she really have dark hair and blue eyes like he imagined, or was she blond and fair skinned? He had no idea.

He wondered if she was still alive and if she ever thought of him. Probably not. In all the years since she left when he was three years old, she hadn't attempted to get in touch with him. What was it about him that made her not love him? He'd struggled with that question all his life and was no nearer an answer now than he had been when he was a child.

His blood turned cold at the fear that Victoria would dislike living at Pembrook as much as his mother had. Victoria said she loved him and promised she would never leave him, but she might change her mind in the future. He would have to make her realize how much he loved her so that she would never want to leave him. He couldn't lose her, too.

seven

Victoria knew the big house at Pembrook would be beautiful, but she hadn't expected its breathtaking interior. She remembered looking at the house from the deck of the *Alabama Maiden* and thinking the only way she'd get to see the inside of such a house was if she worked in the kitchen. Now she was here because the owner of one of the wealthiest plantations in Alabama wished to ask her family's permission to marry her.

From the moment she and her family walked in the front door, she'd been overcome by the spacious rooms and the ornate furniture. She'd almost gasped aloud when Marcus opened the door to the dining room and she spied the long table draped with a white cloth and sparkling candelabras at each end. Even in the daylight, the flickering flames from the candles cast dancing patterns across the wallpaper that Marcus whispered in her ear had been ordered from France by his father. The massive sideboard that sat against one wall had been shipped to Pembrook from England. Her heart fluttered at the thought of sitting in this elegant room at the other end of the table, facing Marcus and presiding over the dinner parties they would give after they were married.

Her uncle swallowed the bite of ham he'd placed in his mouth, laid his fork on his plate, and glanced at Marcus, who sat at the head of the table. "You have a nice home, Marcus. Thank you for inviting us today."

Marcus leaned back in his chair and smiled. His gaze drifted around the room. "My grandfather built the house, but my father was the one who furnished it. I was a small boy during the war, but I've often heard my father talk about how thankful he was the Yankees never came to Pembrook. Of course, he'd hidden most of the valuables. So even with all the slaves gone, he had money after the war to get Pembrook back on its feet. And he did a great job."

Her uncle nodded. "He sure did. Now it's yours, and I'm sure you'll continue to make it successful."

Before Marcus could respond, the door to the kitchen opened, and the woman who'd served their meal stepped into the room and stopped a few feet away from the table. Her dark skin glistened in the candlelight. A red scarf tied at the back of her head covered her hair, but a few tufts of wiry dark hair stuck out over her ears. She stood with her hands clasped in front of her and her gaze directed at the floor.

Marcus glanced at her. "Yes, Sally?"

"I's wond'rin' if ya'll needs anything else, Mistuh Mahcus."

Marcus looked from Victoria to her mother and uncle. "Would you like anything else before Sally serves dessert?"

Victoria's mother laid her napkin beside her plate and smiled at the woman who'd cooked their meal. "No, thank you, but everything was delicious."

The woman didn't look up but nodded.

Victoria turned in her seat to get a better look. "Sally, Mr. Marcus told me that you cook all his meals. He's very fortunate to have such a good cook."

Sally's eyes grew wide, and she darted a quick glance in Victoria's direction. "Thank you, ma'am."

Victoria smiled. "I can only echo my mother's words about how tasty everything was."

Sally opened her mouth to speak, but Marcus interrupted. "You can take these dishes and serve dessert now, Sally."

The woman scrambled to clear the dishes away from the table. In a matter of minutes, she had taken all of them to the kitchen and returned with desserts plates filled with apple cobbler. Victoria picked up her fork, cut into the flaky crust, and took a big bite.

"Mmm." Swallowing, she reached out and touched Sally's arm as she placed a plate in front of Uncle Samuel. "Sally, this is heavenly. I don't know when I've eaten better."

Surprise flashed in the woman's eyes, and she glanced down at Victoria's hand on her arm. Taking a swift step back, she distanced herself from Victoria. "Thank you ag'in, ma'am."

She turned and rushed to the kitchen. Victoria turned a questioning gaze toward Marcus. "Did I frighten Sally?"

He shrugged. "She doesn't talk much. You probably just caught her off guard."

Victoria stared at the closed kitchen door, but the woman didn't enter the room again. When they had finished their dessert, Marcus stood. "If you're through, let's go into the parlor where we can relax. Then I'd like to show you around Pembrook."

Marcus stood at the door and waited until they had all passed by before he stepped in front and led the way down the hallway toward the parlor at the front of the house. Victoria glanced up at the curving staircase that led to the upstairs as they passed and wondered what the rooms up there looked like. If they were anything like those she'd already seen, she knew she was about to enter into a life she never would have dreamed about.

In the parlor, Victoria and her mother sat down on the gilt-framed French sofa that faced a marble fireplace, and her uncle took a seat in one of the sofa's matching chairs beside them. She gazed up at the large mirror above the fireplace and the two pink lusters that sat at each end of the mantel.

She pointed to the lusters. "Marcus, those are beautiful. Where did you get them?"

He glanced up at the enameled, bowl-shaped candleholders with the tier of single-drop crystals hanging toward the base of each stem. "My father had them sent from Bristol, England. Do you like them?"

"Oh yes. They're the most beautiful I've ever seen."

He smiled and then stepped in front of the mantel, turned his back on it, and clasped his hands behind him. Victoria thought he'd never looked handsomer than he did standing there, his gaze almost caressing her face. He cleared his throat. "It's been a pleasure to have all of you here today. But I must confess that I have an ulterior motive in inviting you here."

Her mother looked at Uncle Samuel, who frowned at Marcus. "What is it?"

Marcus held out his hand to Victoria. "Will you please come stand beside me?"

"Yes." Victoria cast a nervous glance at her mother and rose to stand beside him.

Her mother and uncle didn't blink as she and Marcus faced them. Marcus took a deep breath. "First of all, I want to thank you, Mr. Perkins and Mrs. Turner, for letting me visit Victoria in your home for the past few months. During this time, we have come to know each other. I have also developed a deep feeling for Victoria, and she assures me that my affection is returned. I spoke with her last week, and we decided we would bring our wishes to you today." He reached out and clasped Victoria's hand. "I would like to ask your permission to marry her. I promise I will take care of her and provide her with everything she needs in life."

Neither her mother nor her uncle spoke for a moment. Mama licked her lips and let out a long breath. "Marcus, do you love my daughter?"

"I do."

She looked at Victoria. "And do you love Marcus?"

"I do."

Her mother glanced at Uncle Samuel as if she was struggling with an answer. Uncle Samuel stared at her for a moment before he directed his attention back to Marcus. "But you've only known each other a few months. You need more time before you make such an important decision."

Victoria shook her head. "It wouldn't matter, Uncle Samuel. Marcus and I love each other, and that's not going to change whether we marry tomorrow or six months from now."

Her mother directed a piercing look at Marcus. "Do you promise that you will always respect and take care of my daughter?"

"I will."

With a shrug she sank back against the pillows of the sofa. "Then I suppose I give my permission for you to marry my daughter. I hope the two of you know what you're doing."

Victoria released Marcus's hand and leaned down and hugged her mother. "Thank you, Mama. We do know what we're doing."

Her mother's arms circled her shoulders, pulling her tighter, and she whispered in Victoria's ear, "I don't want you to think I'm not happy for you, darling. I am, but it surprised me. You know there aren't many women who could capture a husband as wealthy as Marcus. You'll be well taken care of for the rest of your life. That's always been my wish for you."

"I know, Mama. Being married to Marcus is the best thing I could ever have imagined."

Her mother released her. "Then be happy. When will the wedding be?"

Victoria laughed and glanced at Marcus. "We haven't decided yet. When shall we get married?"

He smiled. "The sooner the better for me. How long do you need to get ready?"

Her mother stood up and grasped Victoria's arm. "Don't rush it, darling. I'm sure the people of Willow Bend will expect a big wedding for one of the county's most eligible bachelors. We have to make your dress and decide what we'll serve at the reception. Then we need to talk to Reverend Luckett and see when would be a good time to have it at the church."

Marcus frowned. "I don't want to have it at the church, and I don't want a lot of people invited. I prefer that we have it in the garden off the terrace at the back of the house. The flowering plants are beautiful this time of year."

"You don't want to invite our friends?" Her mother shot an incredulous look at Uncle Samuel, who hadn't said a word.

Marcus stepped closer to Victoria and gazed into her eyes. "I want this to be our time and your family's. Of course we'll have Reverend Luckett and his wife, and I'd really like to invite Dante and Savannah. But that's all."

Her mother's frown deepened. "But that will only be four guests."

Victoria sighed. It was so like her mother to want a big event. If given the chance, she'd probably plan the biggest wedding Willow Bend had ever seen. She smiled at Marcus and turned to her mother. "Those four people are Marcus's friends, and they're also the only people I know well. I think a small wedding right here where we're going to live is just what I want."

"Very well." The grumbled words told Victoria that her mother wasn't pleased. "But we'll still need some time to get your dress ready."

Victoria shook her head. "You sound like you're trying to put it off." She turned to Marcus. "When would you like to have the wedding?"

"It would be better for me if we have it before harvest. I think two weeks would be best. What do you think?"

Victoria nodded. "That's fine with me." She turned back to her mother. "Two weeks from today we'll have the wedding right here at Pembrook."

Resignation flickered in her mother's eyes, and she pursed her lips. Giving a slight nod, she glanced around the room. "I hope you'll be very happy here, Victoria. This is a beautiful home."

Victoria felt as if she'd burst with happiness. Marcus reached out and pressed her hand into his. She stared up into his face and smiled. "Are you as happy as I am, Marcus?"

"I'm happier than I've ever been in my life. I can't wait for you to really be home with me at Pembrook."

She let her gaze rove over the ornate furniture and the heavy draperies that hung at the windows. It looked like a picture she'd seen in a book once, but this was different. It was going to be her home, and she was going to be the mistress of this grand house.

❧

Marcus had never seen a more beautiful day. Cooler temperatures had drifted into the area overnight, and the July afternoon felt more like a spring day. The shade from one of the big oak trees scattered at the edge of the garden covered the area where he'd placed the chairs for the wedding guests.

From the veranda, Marcus stared across the garden at the guests who'd gathered for the wedding. Victoria's mother sat in a chair, and Tave and Savannah stood on either side of her. As they talked, from time to time one of them would glance at him.

Mrs. Turner's lips pulled into a nervous smile every few minutes. She was trying to be happy about the small wedding, but Marcus knew she would have preferred a big one in town. Savannah and Tave looked just as uncomfortable. Weren't they happy for Victoria and him? His heart sank at the thought that they didn't approve of the marriage that was about to take place.

Dante, who stood next to him, leaned closer and grinned. "Your life is about to change. Are you scared?"

Marcus swallowed and took a deep breath. "A little."

Dante laughed. "You wouldn't be a man if you weren't. Don't worry, Marcus. Daniel and I are here to get you through this."

Marcus swiveled and turned to Dante. "Savannah and Tave look unhappy. Do they not want Victoria to marry me?"

"I don't think they're unhappy. They're just concerned," Dante said. "After all, you and Victoria haven't known each other very long."

"How long did you know Savannah before you married her?"

Dante laughed. "About the same amount of time you and Victoria have known each other."

"Your marriage has worked out well."

"Yes, but even when two people love each other, it takes a lot of work. Do you remember the conversation we had the day you came to me for advice about your feelings for

Victoria?"

"Yes."

"Then you understand why we're all concerned. You're a good person, Marcus, and you've been coming to church. But as far as I know, you haven't accepted Christ as your Savior."

"No, I haven't."

Sorrow flickered in Dante's eyes. "Then I fear for your marriage. The Bible is very clear about the responsibilities of a husband. If you haven't turned your heart over to Jesus, there's no way you can fulfill the role that God has for husbands."

Marcus's face warmed, and he fisted his hands at his sides. "I love Victoria, and I'll always take care of her. You don't have to worry about me."

Dante shook his head. "But I do. I know how difficult marriage can be even when you love a woman with all your heart. Just remember that I'm always willing to help you in any way I can. And so is Daniel."

Marcus gave a snort of disgust. "Yeah, he cornered me and told me the same thing before you arrived."

"Then I suppose there's nothing else we can say to you today except that we'll be praying for you and Victoria and wish you the best." Dante smiled and stuck out his hand. "Don't look so glum. This isn't a funeral. It's a wedding. This should be the happiest day of your life."

Even though Dante's words and those of Daniel earlier troubled him, Marcus knew this was the happiest day of his life. A beautiful woman who said she loved him waited inside the house. It seemed like a dream come true. Soon Victoria would be his wife. She would be a part of Pembrook, and he wouldn't be alone anymore. Almost as if his father stood next to him and whispered in his ear, the thought that Victoria might hate life on Pembrook and want to leave like his mother did flashed into his mind.

Before he could banish the idea from his head, Daniel stepped through the door that led from the house onto the veranda. He stopped beside Marcus and smiled. "Victoria is ready, Marcus. Shall we take our places?"

Marcus gulped and nodded his approval.

With a smile, Daniel clasped his Bible next to his chest and walked to the spot they'd chosen for the ceremony. Savannah and Tave sat in the chairs next to Victoria's mother as the men approached.

When Daniel stopped and faced the house, Dante moved to stand beside Marcus. Taking a big breath, Marcus turned, clasped his hands in front of him, and stared at the door of the house. It opened, and Victoria's uncle stepped onto the veranda before Victoria emerged. She smiled at her uncle and slipped her arm into the crook of his.

Her uncle whispered something in her ear and bent down to kiss her on the cheek. Victoria murmured something before she directed her gaze at Marcus. Her eyes sparkled, and he thought his heart would burst at how beautiful she looked. It had nothing to do with the dress she was wearing or the small bouquet she carried. Instead, it was the connection he felt as her gaze traveled over his face. For the first time in his life, he felt as if someone was looking at him through eyes filled with love.

So that was how love felt. He'd never known, and now he saw it on the face of the woman who wanted to share the rest of her life with him. A chill passed over him, and he straightened.

A woman will break your heart. His father had said that to him many years ago. It couldn't be true of Victoria, though.

He loved her and wanted to make her happy.

He shook the thought from his mind and watched as she walked toward him. When she and her uncle reached him, he turned to face Daniel, who opened his Bible and began to read. Marcus couldn't concentrate on the words for wanting to glance at Victoria, but she kept her attention on Daniel.

" 'Husbands, love your wives, even as Christ also loved the church, and gave himself for it.' "

Daniel's words startled Marcus, and he turned his head to look at the preacher. He frowned. The command sounded as if it was very important, but he didn't understand. Was the Bible talking about the buildings where people met to worship? He'd have to ask Dante to explain this to him later.

For the remainder of the ceremony, Marcus felt as if he was in a daze. He knew he mumbled words promising to love, honor, and keep only to Victoria as long as he lived, and he heard her speak the same vows. He also knew when he slipped the ring he'd ridden to Selma to purchase on her finger, but he remembered little else.

"I now pronounce you man and wife," Daniel said.

Marcus stared down at Victoria's hand that he grasped and then raised his eyes to her face. She was smiling, and he thought he detected a hint of tears in the corners of her eyes. He stared at her a moment, not knowing what to do.

Dante leaned forward and whispered in his ear. "Why don't you kiss your bride, Marcus?"

He hesitated a moment, not willing to break the spell that could hardly make him believe this gorgeous woman had just married him. Then he leaned forward, grazed her cheek with his lips, and whispered in her ear. "I love you more than I've ever loved anyone before, Victoria. I can't tell you how happy you've made me today."

She smiled as he straightened and touched his cheek with her fingers. "I love you, too, Marcus. I'm honored to be your wife."

Daniel stuck out his hand to Marcus. "Congratulations. I hope you'll be very happy."

Marcus shook hands and turned to Victoria's mother, who'd stepped up behind them. She kissed Victoria on the cheek and smiled at him. "I pray you'll have a happy life together."

"As do I," Savannah said and reached out to grasp Victoria's hand.

Tave put her hands on Victoria's shoulders and stared into her eyes. "Remember to put God first in your marriage, and He'll take care of you and Marcus."

Marcus put his arm around Victoria's shoulders and drew her close to him. He looked at the people who'd come to witness their wedding, and his heart swelled with gratitude. Not only did he have a wife; he also was beginning to have friends.

He cleared his throat. "I want to thank all of you for coming to our wedding today." He glanced from Victoria's mother and uncle to the two couples. "I hope that not only Victoria's family but our friends as well will know that our home will always be open to you. Now if you'll come into the house, I believe Sally has baked a cake and has some cider made from apples grown in our orchard."

Victoria looped her arm through his as they walked toward the house. With his free hand, he reached over and covered hers, which rested on his arm. He'd never felt such a protective feeling in his life. He was determined to make her like her new life at Pembrook.

eight

Victoria stretched her arms above her head and wiggled her toes in an effort to wake up. She turned her head to stare at the pillow next to her. The indention where Marcus's head had rested was the only indication that he had slept there. The sun streamed through the big bedroom windows, and she wondered what time it was. From somewhere in the house a clock chimed, and she counted the sounds.

Her eyes grew wide, and she bolted upright in bed. Eight o'clock. She'd never slept that late in her life. Marcus would think he'd married a lazy woman.

She sprang from the bed, ran to the washstand where a pitcher and bowl sat, and poured some of the water for her morning bath in the delicate china basin. She hurried through her morning preparations and ran to the walnut armoire where her mother had hung her dresses yesterday. Pulling out a simple day dress, she slipped it over her head and hurried out of the room.

As she strode down the upstairs hallway toward the staircase, she studied each of the bedrooms she passed. Marcus had pointed out three last night and told her that her family was welcome to stay anytime. The memory of how attentive he'd been to her feelings the night before drifted into her mind, and she smiled. He wanted her to be happy at Pembrook, and she knew she would be.

She reached the staircase and started to step down, but a closed door directly across the hall caught her attention.

She hadn't noticed it the night before, and Marcus hadn't mentioned the room. She wondered what was behind the door.

The smell of baking bread reached her nostrils, and her stomach growled. She'd hardly touched her food last night, and she was hungry. Undecided which to do, she glanced from the door to the direction of the tempting smells.

Curiosity won. She backed away from the stairs, walked to the closed door, and grasped the doorknob. It didn't open, and she pushed harder. Locked. That was the only explanation. Victoria backed away from the door and frowned. Why would Marcus have one of the rooms locked?

The aroma of frying bacon mingled with the baking bread drifted up the staircase, and her stomach growled. Victoria shrugged. She would ask Marcus later.

She dashed down the stairs, hurried to the kitchen, and pushed the door open. "Good morning," she called out as she entered.

Sally Moses whirled around from her position at the dry sink by the wall and gasped. A bowl she'd been in the process of washing slipped from her fingers and crashed to the floor. Sally's wild stare darted from Victoria's face to the pieces of shattered glass at her feet. She shrank against the dry sink and uttered a moan.

"I sorry, Miz Raines. I doan know what make me be so clumsy this morning."

Victoria stopped in amazement at the fear she saw in the woman's face. Did she think Victoria would berate her for breaking a bowl? Victoria smiled and stepped closer. "Don't apologize. It wasn't your fault. I shouldn't have startled you." She glanced around the kitchen. "It's just a bowl. Where's the broom? I'll help you clean it up."

Sally grabbed the bottom of her apron and dried her dripping hands on the fabric. "No'm. I clean it up. You go on in the dinin' room and sets down. I take care of this here bowl after I serves you breakfas'."

Victoria glanced over her shoulder and frowned. "Sit in the dining room? I don't want to sit in there and eat all alone. What time did Marcus leave?"

"Mistuh Mahcus, he leave early ev'ry mo'nin'. He tole me to fix you somethin' to eat when you woke up."

Victoria rubbed her stomach. "I am hungry, but I'm not going in that dining room. I'll sit right here at the kitchen table. That way we can talk while I eat. I want to get to know you better."

Sally bit down on her lip and shook her head. "I doan think Mistuh Mahcus want his wife to be eatin' in no kitchen. Not when you got that big table to set at."

Victoria laughed. "Exactly. It's a big table, and I'm not going to sit in there alone. Now tell me where you keep the plates, and I'll get one out for myself."

A slow smile curled Sally's lip, and she pointed to a cupboard. "They's in there. I'll pour you a cup of coffee whilst you gittin' a plate. Then I'll git you some biscuits and gravy and some bacon."

Twenty minutes later, Victoria pushed her chair away from the table and wiped her mouth on the napkin Sally had handed her. "That was delicious, Sally. I've never tasted biscuits that good. Who taught you to cook?"

A shy smile pulled at Sally's mouth. "My granny be the best cook at Pembrook. She learned me ev'rythin' I know when I was a little girl."

"Did your mother like to cook, too?"

Sally's body stiffened, and she reached for Victoria's dirty dishes. "I doan 'member my mama. Mastuh Raines sold my mama off when I was little."

Victoria frowned. "Sold her. . ." The truth dawned on her. Sally and her mother had been slaves. Victoria raised her hand to cover her gaping mouth. After a moment, she spoke. "Oh, Sally. I'm so sorry. I didn't mean to cause you pain by making you remember the past."

"I reckon I doan never forget it, Miz Raines. It be with me all the time."

"I expect it is. It must have been very hard for you to grow up without a mother, but you're fortunate you had a grandmother. What about your family now?"

"Well, my grandmamma died 'fore the war. When we was freed, me and my husband lived out to the Crossroads for a while. Then when Mistuh Raines start wantin' tenant farmers, we come back to Pembrook. Our son, he born here. Been here evah since."

Victoria smiled. "You have a son? What's his name?"

"James. He a good boy."

"I'm sure he is." Victoria watched Sally carry the dirty dishes to the dry sink and set them in a pan of water. "What can I help you do this morning?"

Sally tilted her head to the side and turned around slowly to face Victoria. A look of unbelief covered her face. "He'p me?"

"Yes. Now that I'm living here, I want to keep busy. How about if I help you with the noon meal? I can cook, although I know I'm not as good at it as you are. And I can wash dishes."

Sally's mouth dropped open wider, and she stared at Victoria. "Miz Raines, you cain't be a-workin' in no kitchen like hired he'p. You the mistress of this here house. Mistuh

Mahcus won't like it for you to be doin' such as that."

Victoria laughed. "Don't be ridiculous, Sally. I worked in the kitchen of a boardinghouse in Mobile. I tell you what I'll do. I'll run back upstairs and make the bed; then I'll come back down here. You find me an apron while I'm gone, and I'll help you with the morning chores."

Sally shook her head. "Miz Raines, I doan think Mistuh Mahcus gonna want you a-workin' with me."

"Oh, he'll be glad I found something to occupy my time. I have to find something to do. I can't sit in a chair all day long." She started out of the kitchen but stopped at the door and turned back to Sally. "I meant to ask you about a locked room upstairs. What's in there?"

Sally lips quivered. "That's Mistuh Raines's room."

Victoria frowned. "Marcus's room?"

"No'm. His father's."

"Why is it locked?"

"Mistuh Mahcus locked it after his pappy died. He doan let nobody in there 'cept me ev'ry once in a while to clean."

Victoria nodded. "I see. Well, I'll be back in a minute."

She hurried through the house and up the staircase to the second floor. When she reached the closed door to her father-in-law's bedroom, she felt an urge to try the door just in case Sally had been wrong.

She grasped the doorknob in her hand and turned it, but the door wouldn't open. Victoria backed away from the door and stared at it. Why would Marcus keep the door locked and forbid anybody to enter? She would have to ask him about that.

❧

Marcus could hardly wait for noon. He'd wanted to stay home with Victoria this morning, but he knew he couldn't.

The work on a plantation as large as his didn't wait for any man, and he had obligations.

As he'd ridden across Pembrook land all morning, checking on the fields of the various tenants, he pulled out his watch from time to time to see how much longer it would be before he could go back to the big house.

Victoria had been sleeping when he left, and he couldn't bring himself to wake her up. He sat beside the bed for a while staring at her and wondering how he became so lucky to get a wife as beautiful as she.

Ever since she'd agreed to marry him, he'd dreamed of how she would look as the mistress of the big house. Now he imagined her sitting in the parlor at Pembrook, maybe some kind of needlework in her hands as she waited for her husband to come from the fields. She would set her work aside, rise from her chair, and glide across the floor to welcome him home.

The thought made him yearn to see her. He pulled the watch from his pocket again. It wasn't yet noon, but that didn't matter. He wanted to see his bride. He turned his horse toward home.

When he arrived at the big house, he tossed the reins of his horse to one of the young boys who worked in the stable and hurried toward the house. His excitement grew as he stepped to the front door, pushed it open, and strode to the parlor.

At the entrance to the room he stopped and stared. Victoria was nowhere in sight. Laughter rang from the back of the house, and he frowned. Turning toward the sound, he moved to the closed door of the kitchen and paused. Victoria's laughter came from inside.

He pushed the door open and stood in amazement at the sight before him. Sally stirred a bubbling pot on the stove, and Victoria, the sleeves of her dress rolled up, was up to her elbows in soapsuds as she washed dishes at the dry sink.

Victoria glanced over her shoulder, and her face lit up when she saw him. "Marcus," she cried out, "you're home earlier than we expected."

"I. . .I wanted to see if you were all right."

She dried her hands on her apron and hurried across the room toward him. He glanced past her at Sally, who had turned to stare at him. She lowered her gaze, faced the stove, and directed her attention back to the cooking food.

Victoria stopped in front of him, stood on her tiptoes, and kissed his cheek. "I'm so glad you're home. Why didn't you wake me up before you left this morning?"

Marcus's heart plummeted at the sight of her. She looked nothing like the vision he'd had all morning. Tendrils of hair had escaped the bun at the back of her neck, and she brushed them out of her eyes. Spots of flour dotted her face, and the apron she wore sported a stain that looked like grease. He pulled his gaze away from her disheveled appearance and stared into her dark eyes. "I wanted you to sleep on your first morning here."

She arched an eyebrow and smiled. "From now on, you wake me up. I want to see my husband in the mornings. It's so sweet of you to be concerned for me on my first day here, but you needn't worry. Sally has taken care of me just fine. In fact, she has a wonderful meal cooked for us."

He glanced at the dishpan. "And you're washing dishes?"

She nodded. "I've been busy all morning. I made the bed, and then I dusted the parlor before I came in to help Sally with the noon meal. I love this house, and I can't tell you how wonderful I feel being here."

"That's good." Marcus looked at Sally again, but she

hadn't moved. He took Victoria by the arm and nudged her forward. "I need to speak to you in the parlor, Victoria."

"All right." She started from the kitchen but stopped and called over her shoulder, "I'll be right back, Sally."

Marcus clenched his fists as he followed Victoria to the parlor. When they stepped into the room, he motioned her to sit in a chair and positioned himself to stand in front of her. She gazed up at him, and his heart pumped. How could he make her understand what he wanted their life to be at Pembrook?

He took a deep breath and raked his hand through his hair. "Victoria, what were you thinking going into the kitchen and working alongside Sally?"

The smile on her face dissolved, and her eyes grew wide. "What are you talking about, Marcus?"

"You are the mistress of this house, Victoria. I want you to remember that."

Victoria pushed up out of her chair. "I thought I was your wife and that my job was to take care of our home."

He blinked in surprise. "You are my wife, but I don't want you acting like the hired help. I don't need another worker. I need a wife who wants to make a home with me, preside over the table at dinnertime, conduct herself like a Southern lady of privilege."

She moved closer to him. "But I want our home to be our own special place. I can't be like a princess sitting on a throne. I have to be active in making our life happy. I'm used to working, Marcus, and I can't change that. Sally is the only woman here, and I want to be friends with her."

He drew back in surprise. "Friends with her? That's impossible."

"Why?"

"Because she's. . ."

"Not white?" Victoria finished the sentence for him.

He licked his lips. "Sally is a former slave who works at Pembrook now. You are the owner's wife. There is no place for friendship between the two of you."

Anger flashed in her eyes. "That's the most ridiculous thing I've ever heard. The war has been over for sixteen years. Don't you know that ended a lot of the old ideas in the South? I worked with women whose skin color was different than mine in Mobile, and I found I liked them. This morning I found that I like Sally. I can't ignore the fact that she's in this house, and I can't sit around all day waiting for you to come home. If we're going to be happy together, you have to let me be the person I've always been. Don't try to change me, Marcus."

"I just think you should remember the difference in your and Sally's stations in life. If you want friends, there are Savannah and Tave."

Victoria crossed her arms and glared at him. "They both live miles from here. How am I supposed to see them?"

"I'll have one of the workers drive you over in the buggy whenever you want to go see either of them. As far as Sally is concerned, you can't be friends with her. My father made it clear that there was a line between the owner and the workers at Pembrook. They're like children that we have to take care of. Remember that when you deal with Sally. Be firm with what you expect from her and don't become involved in her life."

She shook her head. "That's the most ridiculous thing I've ever heard. You sound like a slave owner from thirty years ago. It's a new day in the South, Marcus, and your father is no longer here. You have to make your own decisions and find your own way of dealing with life as it is now."

He regarded her for a moment. "Your mother said you've always been impulsive. For now, I see I can't change your mind. As you get used to life here and see how the tenants need guidance, you'll change your opinions."

She shook her head. "I wouldn't count on it." Her gaze softened, and she reached up and stroked his cheek. "I don't want to argue with you, Marcus. I love you with all my heart, and I want us to be happy. Please try to understand how I feel."

His heart pricked at the sadness he detected on her face. How could he deny her anything? "I want us to be happy, too. I love you so much, Victoria, but you have to understand you've entered a different world." He glanced down at her simple dress and the grease-stained apron. "How would you like to take a trip?"

Her eyes lit up. "A trip to where? You said we couldn't take a honeymoon trip until later in the summer."

"I know, but I've changed my mind. Maybe we need to get away from Pembrook for a few days and go where we can be alone and get to know each other. We could go to Selma and stay at the St. James Hotel, and we could shop for a new wardrobe for you. I want to buy you whatever you need."

She clasped her hands in front of her. "Oh, Marcus, do you really mean it? We can stay in a real hotel, and I can shop for clothes?"

He put his arm around her and drew her close. "You can have anything your heart desires. I want you to know how much I love you and how proud I am to have you for my wife."

"When can we go?"

"How about the first of next week? That should give me time to make arrangements to be away."

She threw her arms around his neck and hugged him. "Thank you, Marcus. I love you."

He put his finger under her chin and tilted her face up. The lips that he'd dreamed about so many nights hovered right beneath his. He tightened his embrace as her arms circled his neck and pulled his head down until their lips met in a sweet kiss.

nine

With only one day left until their departure for Selma, Victoria was determined to finish the dress she'd started working on before her wedding. As she concentrated on the hem, she thought back to how wonderful the last few days had been.

Ever since her argument with Marcus the day after their wedding, she'd tried not to upset him. She was sure that once they had adjusted to living together, he would see how some of the ideas he still held to weren't reasonable.

In the meantime she still helped Sally, but she tried to be waiting in the parlor when it was time for him to arrive home. He hadn't said anything else, and she hoped there wouldn't be another confrontation like the one they'd had.

The sound of music drifted through the house, and she sat up straight. The needle she'd been pushing through the fabric jabbed her finger, and she cried out. A tiny drop of blood bubbled up on her skin. Frowning, she stuck the finger in her mouth in an attempt to ease the sting.

The music echoed through the house again, and she pushed to her feet. What was it, and where was it coming from?

She stepped into the hallway outside the parlor and listened. The sound of a low-pitched voice singing reached her ears, and she moved in its direction. Stopping outside the closed door to the kitchen, she put her ear next to the door and listened again.

Strumming on some kind of instrument accompanied

a melancholy voice that moaned the words of a song like nothing she'd ever heard. " 'The river calls me home, ain't gonna stay no more. The river calls me home, ain't gonna stay no more. When I leave on that boat, it gonna drop me off on heaven's shore.' "

"Oh, that's good, James. You done make up one I like." Sally's voice drifted to her ears.

Victoria pushed the door open and stepped into the room. A young man who resembled Sally sat in a chair, and he held the strangest instrument she'd ever seen. "I heard the music, and I came to see what was going on."

The young man jumped to his feet and backed toward the door that led outside. "I's sorry, Miz Raines. I didn't mean to cause no problem. I jest come in here to wait so's I can walk home with my mama. Whilst I was here, I let her hear my new song. I won't do it no more, Miz Raines."

Victoria held out her hand. "No, don't go. I liked your music." She glanced at Sally. "Is this your son?"

"Yes'm. This be James. He likes to play music. He makes up songs all the time."

Victoria pointed to the instrument he held. "Is that a homemade guitar?"

James nodded. "Yes'm."

Victoria took a step closer and studied the strange device he held. "Would you tell me how you made it?"

James held out the instrument for her to see. "Mr. Perkins down at the store give me a empty cigar box, and I cut me a hole in the middle of it. I found a plank that Mistuh Mahcus done tore off the henhouse, and I whittled it down till I got the right size to nail onto the box for my handle. There was some old screen wire left over in a shed out back, and I made me some strings out of that. 'Course, first I had to make this here bridge to lift the wires up so they'd make a sound."

Victoria's mouth gaped open. "You made this all by yourself?"

"Yes'm."

"James, you're so smart. And the song I heard you singing, did you write that, too?"

"Yes'm."

Victoria ran her hand down the strings and plucked at one of them. The twang sent a thrill through her. "I've heard lots of musicians in Mobile, but I've never heard any song like the one you were singing. What kind of music is it?"

James shrugged. "I doan know. It just a kind of song my mama and pappy used to sing to me when I was a little boy."

Sally stepped forward. "Back when we was slaves, we'd get so sad sometimes we jest had to let out our feelin's in our songs. James's music jest the same kind we used to sing."

Victoria nodded. "It does have a sad sound. It seems to come from the bottom of your soul. I'm glad I heard you singing, James. It was very beautiful."

The front door of the house opened, and Marcus's voice rang out. "Victoria, where are you?"

She whirled around at the sound of her husband's voice. "I have to go now, but please come again and play for me. I've never heard such a haunting melody in my life."

Marcus stood in the middle of the parlor when she reentered the room. He turned and smiled at her. "There you are. I saw your sewing lying here and wondered where you were."

"I was taking care of something in the kitchen." She stopped in front of him and put her arms around his neck. "I can hardly believe that we're leaving on our trip tomorrow. I'm so excited. Did you see my mother when you went to town today?"

"I did. I told her and your uncle that we would be away for the next two weeks. They said to tell you to have a good time."

She tilted her head and directed what she hoped was a coy look at him. "Just being with you will make me enjoy the trip. Of course, the new clothes you've promised me will be nice, too."

He threw back his head and laughed. "Mrs. Raines, you make me so happy."

"And you do me, too, Mr. Raines."

He drew away from her. "I need to go out to the barn and see if I can see James before he goes home for the day. I want him to drive us in the buggy to the boat landing tomorrow. We're going to Selma on the *Montgomery Belle.*"

"Then you don't have to go to the barn. He's in the kitchen."

Marcus stiffened, and he frowned. "You were in the kitchen with him?"

"Not just with James." Victoria picked up the dress she'd been hemming and sat down. "Sally was in there, too. I don't know if they've left to go home or not."

"Victoria, I have told you how I feel about. . ."

She frowned at him. "I wasn't doing anything wrong, Marcus. I heard some music, and I went to investigate."

"Music? What kind of music?"

She shrugged and reached for the thimble she'd set on the table next to the chair. "It was a song that James made up. It was really quite beautiful."

His eyes grew wide. "You were in there listening to music with Sally and James? Really, Victoria, have you not listened to a thing I've told you for the past week? You are to keep your distance from Sally and from James, too. The only conversation I want you having with them is when you instruct them in what you want them to do."

"And what if I don't want them to do something? What if I just want to talk to somebody or to listen to a gifted young man play a homemade instrument?"

He gritted his teeth. "Find something else to occupy your mind. Don't befriend the tenant farmers' families."

She held up her hand. "Let's not start this again. We're leaving on a trip tomorrow, and we don't need to leave with an argument hanging over our heads."

He exhaled. "You're right. But when we get back, we're going to settle this once and for all."

Victoria jumped to her feet, and the dress tumbled to the floor. "Yes, we are."

He stared at her for what seemed an eternity before he turned and stormed to the hallway. Victoria stood with her fists clenched for a moment before she dropped back into the chair. What had happened? One moment she and Marcus were speaking of their love, and in the next instant they were locked in a war of wills. How they were ever going to settle this disagreement she had no idea.

≈

Victoria stared at her image in the full-length mirror of their hotel suite at the St. James Hotel. The new evening dress with its white satin underlayer and pink silk overlay trimmed in pink roses and delicate lace had taken her breath away when she first saw it in the store. The scooped neck and short sleeves added a stunning look to the elegant garment. She'd never felt so beautiful in her life.

The door to the room opened, and Marcus entered. His eyes lit up when he saw her. "You look beautiful."

She bowed her head and curtsied. "Thank you, kind sir.

Maybe I can persuade you to escort me to the dining room tonight."

"It would be my honor." He stopped beside her. "Do you mind if we have guests join us?"

"Who?"

"Matthew Chandler and his wife, Portia. I ran into them downstairs. Matthew's family owns Winterville Plantation, and he and his wife are staying at this hotel, too. They asked if we would join them tonight."

"That would be wonderful," Victoria said. "I'd like to meet Portia. Is Matthew a friend of yours?"

"I hardly know the man. His father is still in control at Winterville. I don't think Matthew stays there much. He met his wife when he visited family at Dauphin Island. They've been married several years."

"They sound interesting, but do you think I'm dressed all right?" She grinned and turned in a slow circle.

His gaze raked her from head to toe. "I've never seen anyone more perfect."

Two hours later, Victoria swallowed the last bite of her dessert, wiped her mouth on her napkin, and glanced across the table at Portia Chandler. She studied the tiny woman who had picked at her food throughout the meal. Victoria thought she had spent more time pushing her food around on her plate than putting any in her mouth.

Victoria leaned forward. "Portia, my husband tells me you grew up on Dauphin Island."

Portia's hand shook as she set her coffee cup in its saucer. "I did. Are you familiar with the island?"

"I am. I'd lived in Mobile all my life until we came to Willow Bend."

Portia nodded, and the long curls that hung from the back

of her head bobbed up and down. "I heard that. You must miss Mobile a lot."

Victoria laughed and glanced at Marcus. "I thought I would, but then I met Marcus."

Matthew Chandler leaned over and circled his wife's wrist with his fingers. Portia's already pale face grew whiter at his touch. "Portia feels the same way. Don't you, darling?"

Portia dropped her gaze to the tabletop and bit her lip. She nodded but didn't answer.

Victoria glanced toward Marcus, but a sudden movement of Matthew's hand caught her attention. Out of the corner of her eye, she saw Portia wince as if in pain, and that's when she saw Matthew's fingers tightening around Portia's wrist.

Startled, Victoria couldn't react for a moment. Then she pushed her chair back and jumped to her feet. "It's getting stuffy in here. Portia, why don't we go up to the balcony on the second floor and get some air. We can sit out there and watch the river roll by while we cool off." She turned to Marcus. "You men can do without your wives for a while, can't you?"

Marcus stood. "Of course. We'll come up later."

"Good." Victoria grabbed Portia's arm and pulled her to her feet. "This will give Portia and me a chance to get to know each other better."

Without speaking, Portia followed Victoria from the dining room, up the stairs, and onto the second-floor balcony overlooking the river. When they'd settled themselves in chairs, Portia turned to Victoria.

"Thank you."

Victoria arranged the skirt of her new dress around her legs. "For what?"

"For getting me away from him."

Victoria reached over and clasped Portia's hand in hers. "I saw him squeezing your wrist. You looked like you were in pain."

Tears stood in Portia's eyes. "I was, but that was nothing compared to what it is sometimes."

Victoria's heart pricked at the sadness lining Portia's face. "I'm so sorry. Is there anything I can do to help you?"

Portia shook her head. "No one can help me. I should have gotten to know him better before I married him. He seemed so sweet and kind when I first met him. Then after we were married, it was too late."

"Have you talked to Matthew about this?"

"Yes, and it's done no good. I even tried to talk to his father, which was a big mistake. I paid a high price for that. Matthew beat me so badly that my eyes were so black I didn't leave my room for a week."

Victoria wiped at the tears in her eyes. "There has to be something you can do. You can't live the rest of your life in fear of being hurt by your husband."

"I don't intend to." Portia took a deep breath. "One of these days I will disappear. When you hear about it, pray for me that I may escape the monster I married."

"I will."

Portia leaned forward in her chair. "And be careful, Victoria. You didn't know your husband well before you married him, either. Take care that you don't end up like me."

Victoria swallowed and nodded. "I will, but you don't have to worry about me. Marcus would never do anything to hurt me."

Portia tilted her head to one side. "I don't know about that. Matthew told me that Marcus's mother left his father because he was so cruel to her. Just watch out." She squeezed Victoria's hand. "Promise me that you'll be careful."

"I promise."

Victoria was still thinking about Portia an hour later when Marcus joined her on the balcony. He stopped beside her chair. "What are you doing out here still?"

She inhaled. "Enjoying the night and watching the river."

He held out his hand. "It's getting late, and I have a big day planned for us tomorrow. It's time we were going to bed."

She grasped his hand and stood to face him. "Marcus, you've never talked about your mother much."

He shrugged. "Because I don't remember anything about her. She left when I was three, and I never heard from her again."

"Did you ever ask your father why she left?"

"I did when I was little, but he always said the same thing. That she hated life in the South, that she didn't love him or me, and that she wanted to go back to her family. After a while I quit asking when I realized that she left and had no desire to ever see me again."

She stepped closer. "But you don't know that for sure. You only know what your father told you."

His lips thinned into a straight line. He stepped to the railing of the balcony and grasped the top with both hands. "My father wouldn't lie to me. He told me why she left. Why are you asking these questions about my mother?" He grasped the railing tighter as he spoke through clenched teeth.

"I thought there might be something that you don't know. Maybe she had a reason for leaving that you don't know about. If we could find her, she might want to come back."

He raked his hand through his hair and groaned. "I don't want to talk about this, Victoria. I hate my mother for leaving, and I don't want to ever see her again."

"But Marcus—"

"No!" He whirled and glared at her. "Don't you ever talk to me about my mother again. It is none of your concern."

Victoria bristled. "Just like being nice to Sally and the other workers at Pembrook is not my concern? It seems that you have very definite ideas about what I can and can't do."

He took a step toward her, but Victoria didn't move. "You're pushing me too far, Victoria."

She lifted her chin. "What are you going to do? Hit me like your friend Matthew does Portia?"

His frown dissolved into a look of total disbelief. "Is that what you think of me? That I would do something like that?" He shook his head. "My father told me that a woman will turn against you. It didn't take you long to do that, did it?"

Panic surged through Victoria as she stared at Marcus. Without realizing it, she had just inflicted a great hurt on her husband. She reached for his arm. "Marcus, I'm sorry. I speak before I think sometimes. I didn't mean to hurt you."

He shook her hand from his arm. "I think I'll go back down and sit in the lobby for a while. Don't wait up for me."

Victoria tried to stop him as he brushed past her, but he avoided her touch. When he walked through the balcony door to the hotel, she collapsed into her chair and released the tears she'd held back.

What had she done? Her mother's words about how impulsive she was flashed into her mind, and she groaned. But Marcus had been wrong, too. He'd treated her like she was an outsider instead of his wife when he'd refused to even listen to her concerns about why his mother left. He seemed to have the idea that what she thought made no difference. Then there was the problem with their differing opinions on how the tenant farmer families should be treated.

She had only been married a few weeks. This was supposed to be the happiest time of her life, but minutes ago her husband had looked at her as if she was a total stranger. Perhaps her mother had been right. She and Marcus might have needed more time to get to know each other, but it was too late to think about that now. For better or worse, Daniel had said, and now she had to find a way to live with those words.

ten

Two months later, the tension between Marcus and Victoria had increased to the point that at times he thought he would go out of his mind. He hesitated on the front porch of the big house before entering. He tried to stay away from home in the fields as much as possible, but today he was hungry. Not just for food, but for the connection he and Victoria had shared during the first days of their marriage. He longed to get it back, but he had no idea what to do.

He put his hand on the doorknob but couldn't turn it. What was she doing today? He longed to see her in one of the dresses he'd bought for her in Selma, but she hadn't worn one yet. Every day she put on one of her plain housedresses and worked alongside Sally in the house even though she knew how much it angered him. He'd even overheard some of the tenant farmers talking about how she'd walked to the fields where they were working to meet them.

Once he'd also seen her coming from the barn when he returned home early. When he questioned her at supper about why she was there, she'd responded that she wanted James to drive her in the buggy to visit Savannah. Her dark eyes had glared at him. "Am I permitted to use the buggy to visit my friends?" she'd asked. He'd mumbled his reply that she was free to use anything at Pembrook and then stormed from the table.

He had no idea how many times James had driven her to see Savannah or Tave, but he felt sure they must know by now how strained the relationship was between the two of them. Her mother and uncle had to be aware of it, too, because he hadn't been to church with her since their argument in Selma. Each Sunday James drove her to the church and waited until she was ready to come home.

She acted like she hated him, and he couldn't understand why. He only wanted to help her understand what was expected of her as the wife of Pembrook's owner.

Marcus opened the front door of the big house and stepped inside. She wasn't in the parlor, so he walked down the hallway to the kitchen. He stopped at the closed door and listened. Victoria's voice drifted from inside.

"James drove me to Cottonwood yesterday to visit Savannah."

"Yes'm. He tole me that." Sally's soft voice was barely audible. "You have a nice time?"

"I did. We sat on their veranda and listened to James play his music for us. He's really a gifted musician, Sally. Savannah thinks so, too."

"I's glad she likes my boy's music. I always thought they was nice folks over at Cottonwood."

"Oh, they are. Savannah has been like a big sister to me, but she told me something that I was sorry to hear."

"What was that?"

"She said that Portia Chandler had run away from Winterville Plantation."

"What you mean runned away? Like she done took off and left her husband?"

"That's right."

"Why she want to go and do a thing like that?" Sally's voice sounded surprised.

A chair scraped across the floor, and Marcus wondered if Victoria had risen to come to the door. He backed away a few inches but stopped when her footsteps didn't come closer. "I told Savannah that I knew why she'd done it. When we were in Selma, Portia told me that her husband was very cruel to her."

"What you mean?"

"I mean that he hit her all the time. She told me that he had beaten her so badly that she was going to disappear one of these days. She asked if I would pray for her when she left."

Sally clicked her tongue in disbelief several times. "Where you think she gone?"

"Savannah said she asked one of the tenant farmers to drive her to town so she could go to the store. When they got there, the *Alabama Maiden* was docked and ready to go downriver to Mobile. She got on board and left. It seems Captain Mills is a friend of her family. So everyone assumes he was helping her get back to her family on Dauphin Island."

"I shore hates to hear that. I cain't imagine no man bein' mean enough to hit his woman. My Ben, he wouldn't never do nothing like that."

"I would hope not. To my way of thinking, any man who would do that deserves to be hung." Victoria chuckled. "But then, my mother thinks I'm too outspoken at times."

Neither woman said anything for a moment. Marcus started to push the door open, but Victoria spoke. "Sally, did you ever know Marcus's mother?"

The hairs on the back of his neck stood up at her words, and he leaned closer to hear the answer.

"I's jest a chile when she come here. I doan 'member much."

"Do you remember if she was pretty?"

"Oh, yes'm. My grandmamma say she 'bout the purtiest white woman she ever done lay eyes on."

"Do you know why she left?"

"No'm. Like I say, I was jest a chile then."

Marcus clenched his fists and backed away from the door. Victoria had told him nothing about Portia Chandler's leaving, but she had told the whole story to a hired worker in their home. Also she had asked Sally about his mother. How could she discuss his mother after he'd told her he didn't want the subject mentioned? Did his feelings mean nothing to Victoria?

He raked his hand through his hair and groaned. Seeing Victoria now wasn't a good idea. They both might say some things that they would regret later on. He turned to leave the house but stopped when he walked by the staircase. A thought struck him, and he turned to stare toward the upper level of the house.

Taking a deep breath, he grabbed the bannister and climbed to the second floor. He stopped outside the closed door to his father's bedroom. He had come often to the room in the past but hadn't entered since his marriage. He pulled his watch from his pocket and stared at the key that dangled on the chain.

He inserted the key in the lock and pushed the door open. A musty smell of hot air and dust tickled his nose as he stepped into the room and closed the door behind him. The room looked just as he'd left it. The carved walnut headboard of the bed reached toward the ceiling with its ornate crown moldings that came from France. The white crocheted cover on the bed had been made by Marcus's grandmother, who'd died when his father was small. He'd only heard his father mention her once and had often wondered what kind of person she'd been and if she was happy at Pembrook.

Marcus walked to the armoire, which matched the bed, and opened the door. His father's clothes still hung just as they had the day he died. He closed the door and walked back to the chair that faced the fireplace and sat down. His gaze traveled up over the marble mantel to the painting of his father.

With a sigh, he settled back in the chair, gripped the arms, and studied the picture. He thought of his stern father and how he had shown little emotion. Whenever Marcus had cried when he was little, his father had ridiculed him for being weak and ordered him to get control of himself. He made it plain that he would tolerate no tears from his son.

His childhood had done little to prepare him for the task of running Pembrook, and his relationship with his father had done even less to give him guidance in being a husband. He closed his eyes for a moment and thought of Victoria. He hadn't known what love was until she came into his life, but their marriage hadn't brought the happiness he'd expected.

He had to do something to make her realize how much he loved her. He pushed to his feet and strode to the door. Before he walked from the room, he glanced back at his father's portrait. *"Women only bring unhappiness into your life."* He could almost hear the words his father had spoken so often.

That couldn't be true. Dante Rinaldi appeared to be a happy man who loved his wife. He wondered what Dante's secret was. Maybe he should talk with him and find out. Marcus hurried from the room and locked the door behind him before he rushed down the staircase.

An hour later, he rode up to the barn at Cottonwood and dismounted. A young boy appeared at the open door of the hayloft. "Is Mr. Rinaldi around?" Marcus called out.

The boy nodded and turned to call over his shoulder. "Mr. Dante. Somebody here to see you."

Dante stepped out of the barn and smiled. "Marcus, good to see you. What brings you to Cottonwood today?"

Marcus's face warmed. How could he speak of his problems to this man who always seemed so self-assured? "I. . .I wanted to. . ."

Dante waited a moment. "Yes?" he prompted.

Marcus glanced up at the hayloft and wondered if their conversation was being overheard. He pointed toward the house. "Can we talk somewhere privately?"

"Of course." He turned and called over his shoulder. "Caleb, I'll be back in a minute." He walked toward the house, and Marcus followed. When they sat down on the veranda, Dante smiled. "Now what can I help you with today?"

"It's Victoria."

Dante settled back in his chair and arched his eyebrows. "Are you having problems?"

Marcus nodded. "She's so different than I thought she would be. She's made it a point to meet all the tenant farmers and their families and even considers them friends. She stays after me to do the same."

"And don't you want to know the people who work your land?"

Marcus straightened his shoulders. "I know them. I work beside them every day, but they can't be my friends. They're workers that I've hired, and all I want from them is an honest day's work."

Dante exhaled and leaned forward. "Marcus, you're young and just starting out to manage the plantation that was built by your father and grandfather. In their time, though, it was different in the South. They had slaves to work their land. I don't think your father ever accepted the fact that the people who came to Pembrook after the war were no longer slaves. He wanted to hold on to that old way of doing things. We can't do that anymore. If we want to be successful on our land, we have to accept the differences of the people who work it or we will fail."

"But Dante—"

Dante held up his hand. "You're talking to an Italian who settled here. Nobody wanted to accept me, and I had to work for years to gain their respect. I was determined that I would do everything I could to help the people on my land be accepted as worthwhile citizens of this country. Without them, we wouldn't have the workforce to plant and harvest the crops we need to keep the land productive. And we wouldn't be able to provide for our families."

Marcus chewed on his lip and frowned. "I never thought of it that way."

"I think Victoria probably sees it the same way. She knows God loves the tenant farmer families at Pembrook, and she wants to show them. Instead of criticizing her for it, you should be thankful you have a wife with a kind heart."

Marcus nodded. "She is kind, but she can make me so angry. This morning I heard her talking with Sally Moses like she was her best friend. She told Sally that Portia Chandler had run away from Matthew."

"That's right," Dante said. "We didn't get to know Portia well. Maybe because Matthew kept her so close to home. Don't make that mistake with Victoria. Love her and honor her as your wife." He paused for a moment. "And don't fault her for being friends with Sally. They spend a lot of time together like Savannah and Mamie do. Savannah thinks of Mamie more like a mother and loves her with all her heart. Victoria needs a woman to be close to at Pembrook. You should be happy that Sally is there to fill that need. All the farmers I know speak very highly of the Moses family. They say that James is a gifted musician."

"That's what Victoria tells me. She never misses a chance to ask him to play for her."

Dante laughed. "The way you're grumbling, you almost sound like you're jealous of the attention Victoria pays that young man. I suppose she does think highly of him. I've noticed that he drives her to church every Sunday. She's made it a point to see that he comes inside and listens to the service. Victoria told Savannah she couldn't stand to think about him not getting to go to church because he had to drive her."

Marcus's eyes grew wide. "He comes inside to the service? What have all the people said?"

Dante shrugged. "I'm sure there are some who aren't happy about it, but Daniel has let it be known that he'll not listen to any complaining about it. Of course James could go to church with his family if you'd drive your wife to church. We've been missing you. I know Victoria would like to have you come with her."

Marcus shook his head. "I don't know about that. I tried it before we married, and it didn't appeal to me. I always felt restless and sad when I left the service."

Dante smiled. "Maybe that's because God was speaking to you, and you weren't listening."

"What would He have to say to me?"

"That He loves you and wants to give you a good life. He's given you a wife who loves you, and He wants to bless your marriage. I remember Daniel reading the scripture at your wedding that tells husbands to love their wives like Christ loved the church."

"I didn't understand that," Marcus said. "How could Christ love a building?"

"It's not the building. It's all the people who are believers. He loved us so much, Marcus, that He died on the cross for our sins. He wants you to love Victoria with that same kind of love, so much that you would lay down your life for her."

"So that's what it means. I do love Victoria. I suppose we just have to come to some agreement about our differences." He sighed and pushed to his feet. "Thanks for your time, Dante."

Dante stood and grasped Marcus's hand. "Anytime you need me, come by. But let me caution you. You need to get your relationship with God right first. Then let God lead you in your marriage."

"I'll think about what you said."

They talked of the crops and harvesttime that was approaching as they walked back to the barn, but Marcus couldn't concentrate. His mind was on everything Dante had said to him today. Much of it he didn't understand. He needed a good relationship with Victoria, not with a God he couldn't see.

He was more confused now than he'd been when he arrived at Cottonwood.

✥

The oil lamp on the table beside her chair cast a yellow glow across the shirt that Victoria was mending. She tried to concentrate on her stitches, but her gaze kept darting to Marcus, who sat in the chair next to her. He'd been reading a book ever since they'd settled in the parlor after supper.

He hadn't said much during their meal or in the hour since they'd left the dining room.

She sighed and directed her attention back to her sewing. Her mind drifted back to her life in Mobile and how happy she'd been working at the boardinghouse during the day and spending her evenings with her mother. At the time, she'd thought her life very dreary, but now she remembered it with a longing that brought tears to her eyes.

Marcus glanced up from his book and frowned. "What was that?"

Startled, she looked up. "What?"

"You were humming."

Victoria frowned. "I was? I didn't realize it. What was I humming?"

"I don't know. It had a sad sound to it, sort of gloomy."

She gave a nervous laugh. "Then it was probably one of James's songs. They're all very melancholy and sad sounding. Sally says it's the kind of music the slaves used to sing when they thought about their lost lives after being brought to this country. They made up the songs they sang, and now James does, too. He says they used to call it blue music; now it's called the blues because of the way it makes you feel."

His gaze searched her eyes. "Is that how you feel here at Pembrook? Blue? Sad? Do you want to run away like Portia Chandler did?"

She gasped. "How did you know about Portia?"

"I overheard you telling Sally."

She frowned. "But I didn't think you came home today."

"I did, but I didn't stay. I had a lot of work to do."

She laid the shirt aside and stared at him. "I have to admit that my beginning here hasn't been what I thought it would be and that sometimes I'm sad because I don't think you love me. But I have never thought about running away like Portia did."

He closed the book he held and laid it on the table. "Victoria, I do love you. It's just that we have very different ways of looking at things. I'll try to be more understanding of your need to help the people on Pembrook land if you will make an effort to understand my feelings about keeping ourselves separate from them. I've never had anyone who said they loved me before, and I want to build a life here for just the two of us."

She shook her head. "That's impossible, Marcus. This house isn't a refuge for you to escape to at the end of the day and expect me to be waiting to offer comfort and love. Try to understand that I am not your mother, and I'm not going to leave you like she did. I want us to build a life together that includes everybody who lives on our land. I want us to be like Savannah and Dante."

"I want that, too."

She smiled. "Then we have a common goal."

He stood, pulled her to her feet, and wrapped his arms around her. Her heart pounded when he stared down into her eyes. "I love you, Victoria."

"I love you, too, Marcus," she whispered.

As their lips touched, she prayed this would be the new beginning she'd been wanting. Only time would tell.

eleven

The rooster's crowing woke Victoria from a sound sleep on a cold December morning. She didn't have to glance at the pillow beside her to know that Marcus was already up and at the barn. Every morning he arose early to do his chores and then returned to the house to have breakfast with her. This arrangement had come about after their uneasy truce months ago when they'd decided to try to build a life together.

Marcus still didn't understand her friendship with Sally and James, but he didn't argue with her as he had done at first. He also had not accompanied her to church again, even though Daniel had visited several times and Dante had also encouraged him. She could only hope that would change in time.

On this cold morning, she snuggled underneath the covers for an extra few minutes before she went downstairs to help Sally with breakfast. Thoughts of Christmas drifted through her mind, and she smiled at the plans she was already making for their first Christmas together. Along with her mother and uncle, they had been invited to spend Christmas Day at Cottonwood with Savannah and Dante. The Lucketts and Tave's father, Dr. Spencer, would also be guests that day. She was secretly glad they had been invited to Cottonwood because Marcus wouldn't expect Sally to be at the big house that day. She would be free to celebrate with her own family.

She smiled when she thought of how close she and Sally had become since her wedding. Victoria had never had a friend like her, and she couldn't wait each morning to see her. By this time, Sally would have the big stove fired up and biscuits ready to go in the oven. Usually the smell of coffee drifted up the stairs, but not this morning.

The clock in the downstairs hallway chimed the hour, and Victoria sat up, a frown on her face. Something didn't seem right. She threw back the covers, jumped out of bed, and dressed quickly. When she entered the dark kitchen, her heart lurched. Sally hadn't arrived, and the stove's embers had burned down during the night.

Marcus would be back for breakfast soon, and there was nothing to eat. After lighting the lamps in the kitchen, she set about to rebuild the fire in the big cast-iron cookstove. Within minutes a fire blazed, and she had ham sizzling in a skillet and biscuits ready to go in the oven. By the time Marcus stopped at the back door to take off his boots, she had breakfast nearly ready.

A surprised expression flashed across his face when he stepped into the kitchen. "Victoria," he said. "I didn't expect you to be up."

"Sally's not here yet, and I've cooked breakfast for us."

He glanced at the food and back to her. A slow smile covered his face. "I do remember you telling me you worked in a boardinghouse. It looks good."

She waved her hand in dismissal. "Anybody can cook breakfast, but I'm worried about Sally. She's always here by this time."

Marcus nodded. "James is at the barn. He said Sally has been sick all night."

Victoria set the platter of ham on the kitchen table and gasped. "What's wrong with her?"

"He didn't say. Just said that she wouldn't be here for a few days." He glanced down at his hands. "I'll go wash up and then come back to eat with you."

"All right. I thought we might eat in the kitchen this morning instead of at that long dining room table. Is that all right with you?"

"That's fine."

She watched him step out to the back porch where they kept the bucket of water with its dipper and wash pan, but her mind was on Sally.

She couldn't concentrate on her food all through the meal, but Marcus ate like he hadn't had anything in days. When he finished, he wiped his mouth and smiled. "With Sally out, I may get to see some of your talents I haven't experienced yet. I can hardly wait to see what you'll fix for the noon meal."

She smiled. "I'll try to surprise you."

He rose and kissed her on the cheek. "You always do. I'll see you later."

Victoria sat at the table after he left and glanced around the kitchen. It seemed so empty without Sally. She pushed up from the table but grabbed its edge as a wave of dizziness swept over her. Her legs trembled, and nausea welled up in her throat. She dropped back into the chair, folded her arms on the table, and laid her head on them. She lay there until the nausea and dizziness had passed. Then she stood.

She would wash the dishes, change clothes, and go check on Sally. Maybe there was something she could do to make her feel more comfortable. As Victoria took a step toward the dry sink, the dizziness returned, and she wobbled. Maybe she should ask James to drive her to the Moses home instead of walking. She would check on Sally and be back in time to fix Marcus's noon meal.

An hour later, though, as Victoria sat by Sally's bed, she

knew her friend needed more medical attention than she was able to give. Sally's body burned with fever, and the pupils of her eyes had no spark in them. Her breathing was shallow, and hacking coughs rattled in her chest.

Victoria tried to recall if Sally had seemed sick the day before and remembered that she had coughed for several days. She had also seemed tired, but she hadn't complained.

Victoria glanced up at James, who hovered nearby. "How long has she been this sick?"

"Ever since she come home yes'tidy. She was real hot and went right to bed."

"Why didn't you come get me, James?"

"I wanted to, Miz Raines, but Mama say I cain't go up to the big house and talk to you whilst Mistuh Mahcus there."

Victoria pushed to her feet. "That's ridiculous. Marcus wouldn't want your mother to suffer." She thought for a moment before she faced James. "We have to take her to the doctor. Can you pick her up?"

James's eyes grew large. "You mean go see the doctor in town?"

"Yes. We need to get her to Dr. Spencer's office right away."

James backed away. "I doan think Mistuh Mahcus gonna like me drivin' his buggy to take Mama to town."

Victoria glared at him. "It's my buggy, too, James, and I'm telling you to pick your mother up and put her in that buggy now, or I'll do it myself. Do you understand?"

James gulped. "Yes'm. I'll do it, Miz Raines."

Victoria grabbed two quilts from the bed and wrapped one around Sally when James scooped her up in his arms. She folded the other one and carried it to the buggy as she followed James outside. She climbed in the backseat and scooted to the far side. "Put your mother beside me, and I'll cover her up with this other quilt. I'll hold her while you drive."

James lifted his mother onto the seat and watched as Victoria tucked the quilt around her. Victoria glanced up. Tears stood in James's eyes. "Thank you, Miz Raines."

She pulled Sally closer to her. "Sally is my friend, James. I want to see that she's taken care of."

He took a deep breath. "I don't reckon there be many white folks 'round here would feel that way."

"You're wrong, James. Savannah and Dante Rinaldi would, and so would Daniel and Tave Luckett."

He nodded. "Yes'm, I 'spect they would, but not many more."

James jumped into the front seat of the buggy, grabbed the reins, and flicked them across the horse's back. Victoria thought about what James had said as they pulled away from the Moses house. She wondered how many people would have ignored Sally and her family's need because of the color of their skin.

She gasped and sat up straighter as a sudden thought flashed through her mind. In naming the people who would have cared, she realized she hadn't mentioned one name— her husband's. Her heart sank at the thought that she didn't know what Marcus would have done.

❧

Marcus had been so surprised when he walked into the kitchen at breakfast and saw Victoria cooking. He had to admit he enjoyed the quiet time spent with her at the big kitchen table as they ate. He could hardly wait to get back home and see what she had cooked for the noon meal.

But when he walked in the back door, the kitchen was dark and the cookstove was cold. Where could she be? "Victoria," he called out. There was no answer.

He climbed the stairs and checked the bedroom. The dress that she had worn at breakfast lay on the bed, and the door to the armoire stood ajar. Why would she have changed clothes in the morning? Maybe James knew.

When he strode into the barn, another surprise awaited him. James wasn't there, and neither was the buggy. With Victoria and James gone and the buggy as well, Marcus realized there was only one place to look for them—at Ben Moses's house.

He jumped on his horse and galloped down the road toward the spot where the Moses family lived. He knew Victoria enjoyed walking and had often walked Sally home after her day at the big house. Why hadn't she walked today if she went to check on Sally?

Marcus spied the horse and buggy outside the Moses house before he even pulled to a stop. Gritting his teeth, he climbed down and strode across the barren front yard to the door of the house. He raised his fist and pounded on the door. "James, are you in there?"

The doorknob turned, and Victoria opened the door. She smiled when she saw him. "Oh, Marcus, I'm so glad you're here. Come in."

He shook his head and backed away. "Come outside and tell me what you're doing here, Victoria."

She glanced over her shoulder and grabbed her shawl that lay on the back of a chair. Pulling it around her, she stepped onto the porch. "Sally is very ill. James and I took her to see Dr. Spencer. He says she has pneumonia."

Marcus's mouth gaped open. "You took her to Dr. Spencer? Whatever were you thinking?"

Her eyes narrowed, and she tilted her head to one side. "I was thinking that she needed to see a doctor. I was right. Dr.

Spencer said she was very ill when we got there. He wanted her to stay at his office, but she refused. He let her come home if she would have someone with her at all times for the next few days."

"How do they think they're going to do that? Ben and James both have work to do. They can't stay here and take care of her."

Victoria pulled her shawl tighter and straightened her back. "I know. I told them I would stay during the day, and they could take care of her at night."

Marcus felt like he'd been kicked in the stomach. "You? Oh no. You're not going to stay here and take care of that—"

"Stop it!" she yelled. "Don't you dare say anything vile against Sally or call her any names that I've heard from others since I've been in Willow Bend. She's been good to me. At times she's been the only one good to me at Pembrook, and I intend to take care of her."

"You're defying me?" he shouted.

"I'm only doing what I know is right. I. . ." She stopped and swallowed before she touched her hand to her forehead. "I—I don't feel well."

Before Marcus could say anything, Victoria slumped. He caught her in his arms before she hit the porch. He sat down and cradled her close to his body. "Victoria, Victoria," he whispered.

James rushed onto the front porch and stared down at the two of them. "What happened to Miz Raines?"

"She fainted. One minute she was fine, and the next she was falling."

"I'll get some water."

James rushed inside and returned with a cup of water. Marcus held it to her lips, but most of it ran down her cheek.

"Was she all right when you went to town?"

James backed away. "I thinks so."

"What do you mean you think so? Did she say anything?" When James didn't answer, Marcus yelled, "Tell me!"

"I heered her talkin' to the doctor 'bout how she been feelin' bad, but I doan know what he say."

Victoria stirred and opened her eyes. She frowned and stared up at Marcus. "Wh–what happened?"

"You fainted." She tried to rise, but he held her tight. "James said you talked to the doctor. Are you ill, Victoria?"

She shook her head and pulled free of him. "No."

"I's glad you fellin' better, Miz Raines. I better go check on Mama."

Marcus waited for James to go inside before he stood and helped Victoria to rise. When she faced him, he took her by the shoulders and stared into her eyes. "Tell me what Dr. Spencer said."

She blinked back tears but didn't waver under his piercing gaze. "I'm going to have a baby, Marcus."

He gasped and let his hands drop to his sides. "A baby? When?"

"In June."

He waited for her to tell him how happy she was, but she clamped her lips together. When she didn't speak, he took a deep breath. "And how do you feel about that?"

She pushed a strand of hair out of her eyes and pursed her lips. "How do you feel about having a child by a wife who you think defies you, Marcus?"

He tried to identify the emotion he saw in her eyes, but it was no use. He didn't know if it was hate, loathing, or anger she felt. He reached out to her, but she backed away.

His hand drifted back to his side, and he turned away. It

was no use. There was nothing he could say that would make her forgive him for the things he'd just said.

As he rode away from the house, he glanced back once, and Victoria still stood on the porch, watching him. His chest felt like his heart had been hacked into pieces. Victoria was carrying his child, and she had looked at him like she hated him the same way his mother must have when she left him.

His father had warned him, and he'd been right. From what had just happened between him and Victoria, it looked like they might be on the same course that his parents had traveled. However, he knew there would be one difference. Victoria would never allow him to keep his child if she left.

❧

On Sunday morning, Victoria hurried from the church and headed to the buggy where James waited for her. She'd almost reached him when she heard her mother call her name.

"Victoria, wait. I want to talk to you."

She stopped and forced a smile to her face as her mother came toward her. "Hello, Mama. How are you?"

"I'm fine, but I wanted to check on Sally. Dr. Spencer told me that you brought her to his office this week."

"That's right. She has pneumonia, but she's better today. I've stayed with her for the last three days, but she insisted I come to church today."

Her mother's forehead wrinkled. "What did Marcus think about that?"

Victoria glanced over her mother's shoulder and spied her uncle coming toward them. "Hello, Uncle Samuel. How are you?"

"I'm fine. Has your mother told you the news?" he asked.

Victoria's eyebrows arched, and she turned back to her

mother. "What news?"

"Your uncle has sold his store."

The news almost sent Victoria reeling. "Sold your store? Who bought it?"

"Henry Walton," he said. "He's one of Dante's tenant farmers. His family used to have a store before the war, and he's always wanted one. We got to talking the other day, and I told him how I would like to retire. The next day he came back and offered to buy me out."

Victoria struggled to overcome her surprise. "B—but how did he come up with the money on such short notice?"

Her uncle chuckled. "Dante Rinaldi loaned it to him."

Victoria's chin trembled as she thought of the difference between Dante and Marcus. "Yes, I can see Dante doing that. But what are you going to do now, Uncle Samuel?"

He glanced at her mother and smiled. "Well, not only me, but your mother, too."

Victoria's stomach roiled. She had a feeling that she was about to hear news that wouldn't be good. "What are you going to do, Mama?"

She reached out and grasped Victoria's hand. "Oh, darling, the most wonderful thing has happened. Captain Mills has been calling on me whenever the *Alabama Maiden* docks, and we've become quite fond of each other. He's asked me to marry him and go to Mobile with him. Your uncle is coming there to live, too."

Victoria's eyes filled with tears, and she shrank from her mother. "But you can't leave me. I'm going to have a baby."

"A baby?" Her mother's high-pitched cry carried across the church yard, and several people turned to stare. She grabbed Victoria and hugged her. "That's wonderful. Of course I'll come back when the baby is born and stay with you for a few weeks. Is Marcus happy?"

"He's happy," Victoria whispered. "When is the wedding?"

"He's arriving when the *Montgomery Belle* makes its upriver voyage next week. We'll be married in Willow Bend and board the boat when it goes back downriver two weeks from now."

"Two weeks?" Victoria's lips trembled. "That means you won't be here for Christmas."

Her mother reached out and grasped Victoria's hand. "No, but if we can have the wedding at Pembrook, we can combine it with an early Christmas celebration."

"Of course we'll have the wedding at Pembrook, but Christmas won't be the same without you there."

Her mother waved her hand in dismissal. "It may seem strange at first, but you're going to Cottonwood on Christmas Day. You'll have Savannah and Tave to spend the holiday with."

Victoria swallowed the lump that formed in her throat. She'd have her friends, but if things didn't change between her and Marcus, he might not even want to celebrate Christmas.

"But I've never been away from you before. I don't want you to leave me here."

Her mother put her arms around Victoria and pulled her close. "Please be happy for me, darling. When your father died, I was sure I'd never love again, but I have." She released Victoria and stared into her eyes. "If I didn't feel you were well cared for, I would never go back to Mobile. But you have a very rich husband and a beautiful home. And now you're going to have a child. What more could you want?"

Victoria bit her tongue to keep from unleashing the pent-up emotions that surged through her body. Ever since

Victoria had been a child, her mother had talked about how she wanted her only daughter to marry well. And to many people it probably looked like Victoria had made a perfect match. In her heart, though, she knew better. Something was missing from her marriage, and she had to find out what it was. Right now, the big house at Pembrook was a desolate place.

Ever since Sally had been sick, Victoria had risen early and fixed Marcus's breakfast as well as something for the noon meal, but she left the house before he came from the barn. Neither of them talked during supper. As soon as he'd eaten, Marcus disappeared into his father's room and didn't come out until the next morning.

Victoria had stopped at the closed door to her father-in-law's old room several times, but she couldn't bring herself to knock. Marcus didn't appear to have any desire to talk with her, and she wouldn't push herself on him.

When her mother and uncle left for Mobile, she would be all alone at Pembrook. Now she sensed how alone Portia Chandler must have felt. Her hand touched her stomach. She wasn't alone. By the summer she would have her child.

Victoria smiled and hugged her mother. "Then we'd better get busy planning your wedding."

twelve

Victoria had never experienced a Christmas like the one she spent at Cottonwood. A tall spruce tree stood in the parlor, its branches decorated with strings of dried fruit, popcorn, and pinecones. Snowflakes that had been fashioned from white paper dangled from the top of the tree to the bottom. Vance had made a great show of pointing out the ones he had cut and those his sister had created.

Victoria settled back in a chair near the parlor fireplace and moaned with happiness as she recalled the holiday meal they'd just devoured. "Christmas dinner was delicious, Savannah, even though I'm sure all of you tired of hearing me talk about my mother's wedding."

Tave shook her head. "I thought it was a beautiful wedding. They looked so happy."

Savannah turned from stirring the logs in the fireplace and smiled. "I was go glad you invited us. Your mother was beautiful, and her new husband couldn't take his eyes off her."

"She did look happy," Victoria said. "I was upset when she first told me she was getting married, but I want her to have a good life like she thinks I have with Marcus."

Savannah's eyes grew wide. "Is there a problem between you and Marcus?"

Victoria fought back the tears in her eyes. "It seems we don't think alike on a lot of things, and I can't do anything to please him. Right now he's angry with me because I've taken care of Sally since she's been sick."

134

Tave scooted to the edge of the sofa. "What kind of problem has Sally's illness caused between you and Marcus?"

For the next few minutes Victoria told her friends how strained her relationship with Marcus was. "Now I'm going to have a baby, and my mother is gone. I feel so alone."

Savannah and Tave glanced at each other before Savannah spoke up. "We thought there was a problem. You seem to think that Marcus is the one at fault, and I'm sure he bears responsibility for some of your problems. But you must remember that there are always two sides to every story. Perhaps you've been so determined to have your own way that you haven't thought about his feelings."

"His feelings? I don't even know how to understand him. He thinks himself so superior to all the people who live on Pembrook land. He can't stand it because I like Sally and James, and he gets so angry if I visit any of the tenant farmers' homes. I've tried to tell him that they are part of the Pembrook family and we need to treat them with respect. He won't listen to that, though. He just says that's not what his father thought."

"My father and his father knew each other," Savannah said. "I can't say they were friends because Marcus's father didn't seem to want friends. He ruled Pembrook and its people with an iron hand. I imagine Marcus had a hard time growing up with a demanding father and no mother. Have you ever thought that he might just want to be loved by someone?"

Victoria's face grew warm. "Well, he has told me that I'm the only person who's ever loved him."

Tave reached over and touched Victoria's arm. "Do you love him?"

She thought about the first days of their marriage and how

happy they'd been. "Yes, I want us to be happy, but we look at life so differently."

Savannah and Tave exchanged quick glances before Savannah spoke. "Victoria, I know you attend church every Sunday, but was there a time in your life when you accepted Christ as your Savior?"

Victoria clenched her fists in her lap and thought back to the day when she was twelve years old and sat in church, listening to a sermon about how God gave His Son for our sins. That day she had asked Christ into her heart and had promised to live for Him. But had she? Her thoughts had centered on herself instead of what she had vowed that day.

"I did accept Christ years ago, but I suppose I haven't really placed a lot of importance on it in my life."

Savannah knelt in front of Victoria. "Then you need to read your Bible and pray. You need to ask God to turn you into a vessel full of His love and help you show it to others, especially Marcus."

Tave nodded. "Marcus hasn't been taught about God's love. Until he understands it and you recognize the importance of it in your life, the two of you are going to see things differently. If you truly are one of God's children, you have the task of bringing your husband to Christ, Victoria, and you can't do it by doing things that make him angry. You have to approach him in love."

"How can I do that when he treats Sally or James or any other worker at Pembrook with a total disregard for their feelings? Am I supposed to smile and bow down to him?" Victoria's nails dug into her palms from her clenched fists.

Savannah frowned. "Of course not. Just remember what Jesus said about turning the other cheek. Without being angry, tell him that you're sorry he doesn't understand how his words can hurt someone. Tell him you love him and that you're going to pray that God will give him a new awareness of how to treat others. Then you have to pray for him."

Tave arched an eyebrow. "Do you pray for Marcus, Victoria?"

She dropped her gaze. "No."

Savannah leaned forward. "Marcus has a big responsibility at Pembrook. Try to look through his eyes and see what his life is like. Examine the way you treat him, and then try to ease the burdens he must feel at times."

Victoria straightened her shoulders and stared at her two friends. "You make it sound like the success of my marriage depends on me."

Tave and Savannah exchanged smiles before they looked back at her. "That may be true," Tave said. "Are you willing to make the effort and see if you can be happy, or are you going to continue the way you have been and remain miserable?"

She didn't move for a minute. Her gaze flicked back and forth between the two women. Tears flooded her eyes. "I want us to be happy."

Tave nodded. "Good. Then renew your relationship with God, read your Bible about what is expected of a wife, and begin to fulfill that role in your home. No more acting like the impulsive child that Marcus married. Be the woman he wants in a wife."

Victoria thought of the Bible that lay on the table next to her bed. It hadn't been opened in months. Her heart pricked as she realized that she had work to do if she ever expected to be happy at Pembrook.

She reached over and grasped the hands of her two friends. "Thank you. This is the best Christmas gift you could have given me."

They squeezed her fingers. Savannah leaned closer to her. "We'll be praying for you, too, Victoria. Your mother may be gone from Willow Bend, but you're not alone."

A new resolve flowed into her heart as she stared at Tave and Savannah. Both of them appeared to have happy marriages, and they wanted the same for her. For the first time she realized that many of Marcus's problems stemmed from the fact that she had neglected her relationship with God. That was something she needed to remedy first. From now on, she would let Marcus see God's love in her actions.

ಶಿ

After the meal he'd just eaten, Marcus drifted on the edge of sleep in Dante's office. The drone of Dante's voice as well as Daniel's and Dr. Spencer's floated around in his mind as if he inhabited the most tranquil place he'd ever visited. His head nodded forward, and he jerked upright. Had someone spoken to him? He glanced around at the three men, who grinned back at him.

"Having trouble staying awake?" Dante's eyes sparkled as he asked the question.

Marcus straightened in his chair and gave a nervous laugh. "Please forgive me. After the good meal your wife served, I couldn't stay awake."

Dr. Spencer rubbed his stomach. "I know what you mean. Christmas at Cottonwood is always a special event. Tave and I have been coming for years, even before she and Daniel married."

Daniel nodded and groaned. "And I always feel like I can't move after dinner. Savannah and Mamie always make everything extra special."

Dr. Spencer turned to Marcus. "Speaking of Mamie makes me think of Sally. How is she doing?"

Marcus shrugged. "All right, I guess. She came back to work this week. I want to apologize to you, Dr. Spencer, for Victoria bringing her to your office."

A look of surprise flashed across Dr. Spencer's face. "Why would you apologize?"

"Because Sally is the wife of one of my tenant farmers."

Anger flashed in Dr. Spencer's eyes. "Haven't you learned anything in the years since the war? I thought I was through dealing with that kind of attitude around here, but maybe I'm not. I treat every sick person who comes to me no matter what color their skin is. You need to take a lesson from your wife and act like you care for the workers at Pembrook. Sally and her family have worked hard to make life good for you. You need to repay them by at least seeing that they get medical attention when they need it."

Daniel reached out and laid his hand on Dr. Spencer's arm. "My father-in-law gets carried away sometimes, Marcus, but he's right. We're all equal in God's sight."

Marcus stared at the two men and then at Dante. "I'm sorry if I've upset you, but I wasn't brought up to feel that way."

Dante leaned forward in his chair and propped his arms on his knees. "I know you weren't. Your father and I had conversations similar to this several times while he was alive, but he never would listen to what I said." He stared at Marcus for a moment. "Do you remember the warning I gave you last summer at the church picnic about the grumbling I'd heard from your tenant farmers?"

"Yes."

"They talk to the men who live at Cottonwood, and they love and respect Victoria very much because she cares about them. They don't respect you, Marcus, because they say you're trying to run the plantation with the same stern manner your father used. It's a new day in the South, and all they want is to be treated fairly and appreciated for what they do for you." Dante took a deep breath. "The same way that Victoria needs to be appreciated."

Marcus jumped to his feet. "You don't know anything about what goes on between my wife and me. I've given her everything a woman could want—a home, more clothes than she can ever wear, freedom to visit her friends anytime she wants. And what does she do? Defy me at every turn."

Daniel and Dante both rose. Daniel sighed. "We're not condemning you. We want to help you. The two of you seemed so in love when you married."

"I do love her."

Dante studied him a moment. "I think you do, Marcus, in your own way, but not in the way Christ meant for men to love their wives. Do you want to have a good marriage?"

"Yes."

"Then you have to come to understand several things," Daniel said. "First of all, you have to realize that God loves you and wants to give you peace and happiness, but you have to come to know Him. When you do, you'll begin to see people differently than how you view them now, and you'll understand how God wants you to be a better husband to Victoria."

"Dante, you've talked to me about accepting Christ before, but I've never seen a need for it." Marcus struggled to control his anger. "Do you think I'm a bad husband?"

Dante shook his head. "I don't think you're a bad person, Marcus. I believe you want to do what's right, but you don't know how. When you come to the point that you recognize the need for Christ in your life and ask to be forgiven for your sins, you'll see a whole new world open up to you."

"But I don't know how to do that."

Daniel smiled. "I have a Christmas present for you, Marcus." He walked over to Dante's desk and picked up a Bible. "I brought this for you today. I've marked passages that I want you to read. They'll help you understand how Christ loved you so much that He died on the cross for you."

Marcus chuckled. "You make it sound like He died just for me."

Daniel nodded. "He did. The Bible tells us to believe on the Lord Jesus Christ, and He'll come into our hearts and never forsake us." He handed the Bible to Marcus. "Read the passages I've marked, over and over until you understand that kind of love. Then read the places I've marked about how husbands should love their wives. It will all become clear to you. Will you do that?"

Marcus hesitated a moment before he reached for the Bible Daniel held. "I will."

Dante smiled. "Good. And one more thing. When you feel like Victoria doesn't understand your point of view, don't get angry. Be patient and tell her that you love her and try to explain why you feel the way you do. Communication is so important in marriage."

"Marriage is difficult under the best of circumstances," Daniel said. "It takes a lot of work and a lot of compromise to understand how the other person feels. Now that you're going to be a father, you're adding new responsibilities. You want your child to have a happier childhood than you did, don't you?"

For the first time it struck Marcus how his life was about to change. He would have a child who would look to him for all his needs. He thought of Dante and how Gabby and

Vance adored their father. He wanted that, too, with his son or daughter. He didn't want his child to experience what he had growing up.

"Yes, I want my child to be happy."

Dante pointed to the Bible in Marcus's hand. "You have the guide right there that can help you solve every problem you encounter. It's not always easy, but once you turn your life over to God, He'll be there with you."

Marcus stared at the Bible. He'd never had one before. What would his father think of his reading the book? It didn't matter. He had to do something to repair the damage he and Victoria had done to their marriage. And they had to try to make Pembrook a happy place for the child they were going to have.

Maybe Dante and Daniel were right. Reading the Bible might be a start, but he didn't have much faith that it would work.

&

On Christmas night, Victoria sat in the parlor of her home alone. Marcus had disappeared into his father's old room shortly after they'd eaten a light supper, and she hadn't seen him since. That was two hours ago.

During her time alone, she'd thought of everything Savannah and Tave had talked to her about today. She had even brought her Bible down from upstairs and sat in the parlor, reading as she tried to find a way to try to reach her husband. As she flipped idly through the pages, a passage in Hebrews caught her attention, and she read it. When she finished, she reread the passage. *"Let us hold fast the profession of our faith without wavering; (for he is faithful that promised;) and let us consider one another to provoke unto love and to good works."*

The verses made her heart sink. She had not held fast to her profession of faith. Instead, she had married a man who didn't share her beliefs and didn't understand her love and concern for other people.

How many times in the last months had she berated Marcus because he didn't agree with her instead of telling him of God's love for him? Her impulsive manner and sharp tongue had displayed no kindness. Guilt for her actions flowed through her. She clasped her hands and bowed her head.

"Oh God," she prayed, "help me to be kinder to my husband. Tell me how to show him Your love through my actions. I promise You, Lord, from this day forward I will hold fast to my profession of faith. Give me the words and the actions to show Marcus Your love."

She raised her head and thought of Marcus alone in his father's room. What did he do all the hours he spent there? Laying the Bible aside, she rose from the chair and walked to the staircase. Her knees trembled as she put her foot on the first tread and lifted her head to stare toward the upper floor of the house. She took a deep breath and mounted the stairs.

When she arrived at the closed door to her father-in-law's room, she raised her clenched fist and knocked. "Marcus, are you in there?"

Through the paneled door, she heard the sound of footsteps approach, and the door swung open. Marcus's eyes held no emotion as he stared at her. "Victoria, what do you want?"

She breathed a silent prayer that God would give her the words to speak to her husband. She smiled. "I wanted to tell you what a wonderful Christmas our first one together was. I enjoyed the day at Cottonwood, and"—she reached to the collar of her dress and touched the brooch she'd pinned there—"I love my Christmas present from you. I've never had a piece of jewelry as beautiful, and I wanted to thank you again."

He gazed at the brooch for a moment before he looked into her eyes. "And I liked the socks and scarf you knitted for me."

"I hope so. Even in Alabama it gets cold on January mornings. I thought some heavy socks and a scarf around your neck might help you stay warm."

A small smile pulled at his lips. "Thank you for thinking of me."

She blinked back the tears that wanted to fill her eyes. "I think about you all the time, Marcus. You may not believe that because of the way I act sometimes. I warned you before we were married that I was impulsive, and I know I've said things to hurt you. I'm sorry for that. I hope you'll forgive me."

His eyes grew wide. "You want me to forgive you?"

She moved closer to him. "Yes. I haven't been as thoughtful of you as I should be. After all, you're the most important person in the world to me. I love you, Marcus, and I want us to be happy."

He reached out and took her hand in his. "I want that, too. I haven't been as understanding of you as I should have been, and I'm sorry about that. But I do love you, Victoria, and I'll try to be a better husband." He glanced over his shoulder, but she couldn't see what he was looking at. "Dante and Daniel gave me a Bible today with some passages marked for me to read. I've been trying to understand them, but so much of it is strange to me."

"I've been reading my Bible, too. Maybe if we studied it together, we could discuss it and see what God wants to tell us."

His grip tightened on her hand. "I don't know anything

about God. Will you help me learn?"

A tear slid down her cheek. "That's what I should have been doing all along instead of arguing with you because we didn't think alike. I want you to know God."

"Thank you."

She reached up and caressed his cheek with her hand. "Marcus, I miss you so much at night. Do you have to sleep in your father's room?"

He pulled her hand to his mouth and kissed her palm. "Do you want me to come back to our bedroom?"

"Yes."

He wrapped his arms around her and pulled her closer. "I never should have left. Please forgive me for that. I want to be with you all the time."

"I want that, too."

"Wait a minute." He released her, walked back into the room, and blew out the oil lamp on the table. When he stepped back into the hall, he held a Bible in his hand. He wrapped his free arm around her shoulder and smiled down at her. "This is the best Christmas I've ever had."

Her heart pounded in her chest as she stared up at him. "Me, too. But something tells me this is just the beginning for happier times at Pembrook."

thirteen

On a June afternoon six months later, Victoria stepped onto the veranda of the big house at Pembrook, put her hands in the small of her back, and stretched. She'd stayed in bed longer this morning, secretly enjoying the first pangs of impending labor.

She hadn't told Marcus of her discomfort before he left because the baby wasn't due for two more weeks, and he had too much to do in the fields to spend his time worrying about her. Besides, Sally was with her, and her mother would arrive in three days on the *Alabama Maiden* to spend a few weeks. This morning, however, she waited, enduring the erratic pains that had come and gone since early morning, until she could be sure it was time to send for Dr. Spencer.

Now as she lifted her face to the warm sun, she thrilled at the thought that her baby would be born today. She could hardly wait to hold him. She'd been sure from the first that it would be a boy, but Marcus said he'd be happy with a girl.

She smiled as she thought of all the changes that had taken place at Pembrook since Christmas night when she and Marcus had started on their journey of reconciliation. They had carried through on their decision to study the Bible and had devoted several hours each night to reading and discussing God's Word. That time spent together had repaired the brokenness of their marriage, and she treasured those moments.

Over the past months, she had grown in her understanding of the importance of God in one's life, and Marcus had slowly come to an awareness of his need for God. Her happiest moment had come a few months before when he had finally accepted Christ. As a new believer, he spent a lot of time talking with Daniel as his new way of looking at life took root in his soul.

His continued remote attitude toward the tenant farmers and their families hadn't improved, and that worried her. Sally and James were the exceptions. For the past few months, he'd seemed to come to an appreciation of all they did for Pembrook. Perhaps the absence of Victoria's mother had made him understand how important Sally's attentive care of Victoria was to her. He also had come to understand Victoria's love of James's music.

In February when Victoria had mentioned how she wished James had a real guitar, Marcus had told her to order one from Montgomery if she liked. James had been overwhelmed when the instrument arrived, and he'd spent hours ever since playing for Victoria.

A disappointment to Victoria had been the departure of two families from Pembrook. One had taken Henry Walton's place at Cottonwood, and the other one had gone to Oak Hill. Marcus had soon found other tenants to take their places, but she sensed he was saddened by the loss of the two families who'd been there for years.

She had prayed about it and had received peace about the problem. In her heart she knew it was just a matter of time until Marcus would be able to let go of the old ideas of the past and would embrace all the residents of Pembrook as he had Sally and James.

Victoria closed her eyes and inhaled the sweet smell of the roses that bloomed beside the house. Life had never been sweeter, and she'd never been happier.

"Miz Raines, you out here?" Sally's voice from the back door caused her to turn.

"I'm here, Sally. What is it?"

"I don't need nothin'. Just wanta keep my eye on you. Now doan you go wand'rin' off nowheres. I done promised Mistuh Mahcus I be lookin' out for you."

Victoria laughed. "I'm not going anywhere. I just came out for a breath of air."

Sally stepped onto the veranda and studied Victoria. "You feelin' all right?"

Victoria rubbed the small of her back again and frowned. "I don't know. I'm having some pain in my lower back."

"Show me where you hurt." Sally's eyebrows pulled down across her nose.

"Right here. It's—" Victoria's mouth dropped open, and she placed her hand on her stomach.

"Miz Raines, what the matter?"

"I—I just had my first hard contraction," she stammered. "I guess it's time to send for Dr. Spencer."

Sally took her by the arm and guided her to a chair on the veranda. "You sit down right here. I gonna run to the barn and tell James to get Mistuh Mahcus. Then I'll git you in bed. I be back 'fore you knows it."

Victoria eased into the chair and watched as Sally hiked her skirt up and ran toward the barn. She couldn't help but giggle at Sally's long legs skimming across the ground. She looked up into the sky and said a prayer of thanks. It wouldn't be long before she'd be holding her baby, and she couldn't wait.

❧

Marcus sat beside the bed where Victoria lay and held her hand. His heart thumped so loudly in his chest he was afraid she might hear, but she didn't seem to notice. The clock in the downstairs hallway chimed, and he bit down on his lip. James had left to get Dr. Spencer hours ago, and he hadn't returned. What could be keeping him?

"Why didn't you tell me you weren't feeling well before I left this morning?" he asked.

Victoria ran her thumb over the top of his hand. "I knew you had a lot planned today. I didn't want to upset you before I knew for sure what was happening."

On the other side of the bed, Sally wrung the water from a cloth and mopped Victoria's face. "This here gonna make you feels better, Miz Raines."

Victoria gasped and squeezed his hand. After what seemed an eternity, she relaxed and smiled at Sally. "Thank you, Sally. That feels good."

Sally nodded. "I 'member what I feel like when my James born. Now doan you worry none. Sally gonna be right here wit' you till that little baby git here."

"Thank you, Sally. I don't know what I would do without you." She turned her head and smiled at Marcus. "And thank you, too, for sitting here beside me. I feel bad that you had to come home."

He leaned forward and kissed her on the forehead. "And where else do you think I'd be? I gave James instructions he was to come for me the minute anything happened. I'm going to stay with you until Dr. Spencer gets here. Then I imagine he'll make me leave. But for now, I'm right where I want to be."

She smiled. "And where I want you to be."

The front door of the house opened, and Marcus could hear footsteps on the stairway. "I believe Dr. Spencer has arrived."

Sally rushed to the bedroom door and opened it just as the doctor appeared in the doorway. He strode into the room, set his bag on the floor beside the bed, and bent over Victoria. He took Victoria's hand and smiled down at her. "Sorry it took me so long to get here. I was out on another call, and James had to wait until I returned. But I'm here now and ready to go to work. Are you ready to become a mother?"

"I am. I've been waiting for this day."

"Then let's see what's happening here." He looked over at Marcus. "It's time for you to say your good-byes for a while. Sally and I will take over now. Go on downstairs and wait in the parlor while I examine Victoria. I'll come down in a little while and tell you how things are going."

"All right." Marcus stood and leaned over Victoria. "I won't be far away."

She smiled up at him. "I'll be fine. I'll see you later."

As he gazed down at her, the reality of what was about to take place filled him with a fear like he'd never known in his life. Victoria was about to endure pain and suffering like she'd never known, and he was scared. Masking the terror that filled his heart, he bent over her again and kissed her on the cheek. "I love you."

She gazed up at him, and in her eyes he saw love shining for him. He'd never seen that from another person, and suddenly he wanted to do anything he could to make what she was about to endure easier. But he couldn't. All he could do was pray to the God he was just getting to know.

An hour later at the sound of footsteps on the staircase, Marcus rushed to the parlor door. Sally stopped at the bottom as he approached. She grasped the bottom corner of her apron and rolled the fabric between her fingers.

"What's wrong? Where's Dr. Spencer?" Marcus asked.

She pointed upstairs. "He still with Miz Raines. He done asked me to go find James."

"Find James? Why?" Sally tried to step around him, but he blocked her way. "Sally, what's the matter? Why does he want James?"

"He want James to go fetch Miss Tave over to here. He say she done helped him birth babies before, and he need her. He say the preacher can sit wit' you." She backed away. "I's got to go, Mistuh Mahcus. He say I need to hurry."

Marcus stepped aside. "Of course. Tell James to saddle the fastest horse and ride to Daniel and Tave's house as quickly as he can."

"Yas, suh. I will."

When Sally disappeared out the door, Marcus looked up at the staircase landing. He had to find out what was going on up there. He stepped onto the first tread and then hesitated. Dr. Spencer was alone with Victoria at the moment, and he didn't want to pull him away from her. With a sigh he stepped back to the hallway and reentered the parlor.

The Bible he'd been reading at night with Victoria lay on a table beside one of the chairs, and he picked it up. For now all he could do was place Victoria and Dr. Spencer in God's hands. He opened the book and began to read.

It was only a few minutes before he heard Sally rush back up the stairs, but Dr. Spencer didn't appear in the parlor for another hour. When he did, he stopped at the door. "Marcus, may I speak to you for a moment?"

Marcus closed the Bible and pushed to his feet. His heart sank at the worried expression on Dr. Spencer's face. "Of course. Come in."

Dr. Spencer walked into the room and stopped in front of him. "I'm sorry I haven't gotten down here sooner, but I've been busy." He motioned to the chairs. "Why don't we sit down?"

Marcus's body trembled in fear of what Dr. Spencer was about to say. He dropped into a chair, and Dr. Spencer sat down facing him. He scooted to the edge of the seat. "Most times babies are born without any problems at all, but sometimes something that no one expected happens. I'm afraid we have a problem."

Marcus grasped the arms of the chair and squeezed. "What kind of problem?"

Dr. Spencer exhaled. "The baby is breech, Marcus. Do you know what that means?"

He swallowed back the fear that knotted his stomach. "Yes. I've seen calves that are breech."

"I'm sure you have, and you probably know that there are several ways this can occur. In Victoria's case, the baby is lying crosswise instead of head down as he should be."

The words pounded into Marcus's head. The vision of the cow that had died giving birth flashed into his mind. "What are you going to do?"

"I have tried several times to turn the baby, but I haven't had any luck. I don't want to try too often because it's hard on Victoria. Of course, we're just in the beginning hours of labor. I may be successful later."

"And if you're not?"

Dr. Spencer's mouth pursed. "Let's not talk about that. For now I'll concentrate on keeping Victoria as comfortable as possible and see what happens. I've sent for my daughter. She's helped me at times with problems such as this. I also told Sally to ask James to go to Cottonwood and bring Mamie. She's assisted many women in childbirth. I imagine Savannah will come with her. So you will probably have some company before long."

"That's all right. Maybe it will keep my thoughts occupied."

"Would you like to see Victoria before everybody gets here?"

Marcus jumped to his feet. "Yes."

He followed Dr. Spencer up the stairs and into the bedroom. As he walked to the bed, he glanced at Sally, who was still applying cool cloths to Victoria's head. He nodded to her as he bent over Victoria.

"Victoria, are you awake?"

Her eyelids fluttered open, and she smiled. She reached up and grasped his hand. "Marcus, you came back to see me. I'm so sorry you're all alone downstairs while Sally and Dr. Spencer are with me. Are you making it all right by yourself? If you're hungry, Sally can go downstairs and fix you something to eat."

"I'm not hungry, Victoria." Her concern for his welfare brought tears to his eyes. "Don't worry about me. You just concentrate on getting our child here."

She smiled and closed her eyes. "I will. I can hardly wait."

Her face contorted into a mask of pain, and her head thrashed on the pillow. Her groan chilled his blood, and he whirled around toward Dr. Spencer. "What's happening?"

Dr. Spencer stepped forward. "It's another contraction. You'd better go now."

Marcus stumbled to the door but looked back at his wife writhing on the bed. With tears streaming down his face, he ran from the room and down the stairs. He slammed the parlor door and fell to his knees.

"Oh God," he cried, "don't make her suffer like that. Please help her deliver that baby."

He prayed for long minutes, but his heart received no

answer. He relived every cross word he'd ever said to her and begged God to forgive him and give him a chance to make her happy. Finally, exhausted, he rose from his knees, slumped in a chair, and pulled his watch from his pocket.

Six o'clock. According to what Victoria told him, she'd already been in labor twelve hours. How much longer could this last?

❧

Marcus's question hadn't been answered at midnight. Nothing had changed in Victoria's condition according to Dr. Spencer.

He sat in the kitchen, his elbows on the table and his hands on either side of his head. Dante poured a cup of coffee and set it in front of him. "Drink this, Marcus."

Across the table, Daniel nodded. "You need to eat something, too. Sally and Mamie fixed a good supper, but you hardly tasted anything."

"I can't eat," he protested. "Not with Victoria up there dying."

Dante slid into the chair next to him. "Dr. Spencer hasn't said she's dying."

He straightened and looked from Dante to Daniel. "We've worked with animals all our lives. You know as well as I do what happens when one of our animals can't give birth. They die, just like Victoria is going to." He burst into tears and covered his eyes with his hands. "Why is God doing this to us? I thought you said when I became a believer, He'd take care of me."

Daniel reached over and grasped Marcus's shoulder. "I said God would be there with you even during the tough times. We don't know what God's plan is for Victoria. Right now we have to trust that He's going to make things right in the end."

Marcus jumped to his feet, and his chair clattered backward to the floor. "In the end? What does that mean? I don't think God cares. I think He's punishing me for all the years I ignored him, and now He's going to take my wife and child to pay me back."

Daniel and Dante both stood. Daniel shook his head. "God's not in the business of paying people back for their mistakes. He wants to give them hope for the future. Victoria would be upset to hear you talking this way."

"God's here for you, Marcus. You just have to open your heart to His comfort," Dante said.

Marcus shook his head. "Then where is He? I haven't. . ." He paused and tilted his head to one side. "What's that?"

Dante frowned. "What?"

"That singing. Don't you hear it?"

The three of them stood silently for a moment before Marcus strode from the kitchen. "Somebody is singing in front of the house. Who is it?"

He rushed to the front door, threw it open, and stepped onto the front porch. He stumbled to a halt and stared wide-eyed at the scene in front of him. The Pembrook tenant farmers, their wives, and their children stood in the front yard, their faces lit by the lanterns they carried. James stood at the front of the group and strummed his new guitar as the people lifted their voices in song.

A haunting melody rose from the assembled crowd as they sang of a chariot that would come and take them home. The singers stared at the ground, and their bodies swayed in time to the music that seemed to flow from the depths of their souls. Marcus moved slowly down the steps until he stood by James, who played as if he were in his own world.

When the song ended, Ben Moses stepped forward,

his hat in his hand. "We doan mean to be causin' you no problem, Mistuh Mahcus, but we come 'cause we hear Miz Raines ain't doin' too well."

"No, she isn't, Ben."

A low moan rippled through the crowd, and Marcus let his gaze travel over the group. Ben cleared his throat. "Miz Raines been mighty good to all of us ever since she come to Pembrook. My Sally might of died if'n she hadn't taken her to the doctor." He pointed to one of the men. "And Charlie there, his little girl been larning how to read 'cause Miz Raines been a-helpin' her. And when Lester's wife be sick, she done come day after day and brung them food to eat. And she's done lots more. Too much to tell, I reckon. She been there for us when we needed her, and we jest wants her to know we's here for her."

Ben's words stunned Marcus. Victoria had never told him all the things she'd done for his tenant farmers. Now as he stared at them in amazement, he realized how much they loved her. He remembered the day that she arrived in Willow Bend. As he'd ridden into town with James, he'd wished that he had a relationship with his tenant farmers like Dante had with his. Now he realized that God knew that day what he needed to do to make his wish come true, and He had sent the answer in the woman who arrived on the *Alabama Maiden*.

Tears filled his eyes, and he reached out his hand to Ben. The man stared at it for a moment before he grasped it. "Thank you, Ben, for telling me what my wife means to all of you."

"You welcome, Mistuh Mahcus."

Marcus faced the crowd. "I want to thank all of you for coming tonight. This means more to me than you'll ever know. I hope to show you in the days ahead how much I appreciate this and all you've done at Pembrook. Without you, it wouldn't be the great plantation it is. Now take your children home and get some sleep. I'll see you tomorrow."

Ben shook his head. "Nah, suh, I 'spects we be stayin' right here 'til we know 'bout Miz Raines."

"But that could be all night."

"That's all right," Ben said. "We gonna sit right here and pray for Miz Raines. You can come out and tell us when she out of danger."

"B—but it's cool, and there are children here. If you want to stay, come in the house where it's warm."

"Nah, suh. We be all right out here."

Marcus glanced around and saw the determination on the faces of everyone. "Very well. Thank you for your prayers. I'll come outside as soon as I know anything."

He walked back onto the porch where Dante and Daniel waited. "I just realized that God has been here all along. I just haven't been able to see Him."

Entering the house, he saw Sally and Mamie waiting in the hallway. "Sally," he said, "please round up every quilt and blanket you can find and take them to the people outside. I don't want them to be cold. And make sure that everyone has plenty of food and water as long as they are here."

A slow smile spread across Sally's face. "Yas, suh, Mistuh Mahcus. Doan you worry. Sally gonna take care of ev'rythin'."

He didn't know what was going to happen, but he did know one thing. God hadn't deserted him, and whatever happened, He would be there with him.

fourteen

The clock in the hallway chimed six o'clock, and Marcus jerked awake. Daniel snored on the parlor sofa, and Dante lay on the floor. Marcus had no idea how long he'd slept, but it couldn't have been more than a few hours. He'd looked out the window at three o'clock, and the yard was still filled with people.

He stood up and tiptoed to the window. A look outside told him that no one had left. He rubbed the back of his neck and sniffed. The smell of coffee drifted into the room. He followed the tantalizing aroma to the kitchen, where Sally and Mamie appeared hard at work preparing breakfast for everyone.

Sally looked up from rolling out biscuit dough when he walked in. "Mistuh Mahcus, kin I gits you somethin'?"

"No thanks, Sally. I smelled the coffee and thought I'd get a cup."

She turned to walk across the kitchen. "I'll wash my hands and git it."

He held up a hand to stop her. "There's no need to stop what you're doing. I can get it."

Sally cast a surprised glance at Mamie and returned to her work. When he'd poured the coffee, he walked back to the hallway but stopped at the sight of Dr. Spencer coming downstairs. He set the coffee cup on a table and met him at the bottom of the steps. "What is it? Has something happened?"

Dr. Spencer shook his head. "No, but I need to talk with you, Marcus. I think we have to do something."

Marcus grasped the end of the bannister to support his shaking body. "What?"

Dr. Spencer motioned him into the parlor. As they entered, Daniel and Dante both opened their eyes. Daniel sat up on the couch, and Dante jumped to his feet. "Is something wrong?" Daniel asked.

Dr. Spencer shook his head. "I need to talk to Marcus. Maybe you two should leave."

Daniel stood up, and both turned to leave. Marcus held out his hand. "No, don't go. You've been with me through this ordeal, and I want you to hear what Dr. Spencer has to say."

Dr. Spencer took a deep breath. "Very well. I've tried and tried to turn the baby, but it won't move. Every time I do, it weakens Victoria. I don't think she can stand much more of this. She's been in labor for twenty-four hours now, and she's almost to the point of wanting to give up. This concerns me."

Marcus's heart felt like ice. "Give up? You think she wants to die?"

"I'm afraid so if something doesn't happen soon."

"What else can you do?" Marcus asked.

Dr. Spencer hesitated before he spoke. "I haven't mentioned my last option yet, and I'm not sure I even want to use it. But it may be the only way to save at least one of them. If something doesn't change, we're going to lose Victoria and the baby."

Marcus heard the words, but he couldn't move. Lose Victoria and his child? *Please, God, don't let that happen,* he prayed. He took a deep breath. "Then what's our last option?"

Dr. Spencer chewed on his lip before he spoke. "I recently read about an operation that a doctor in Tippecanoe County,

Indiana, performed about a year and a half ago. The woman couldn't give birth, and the doctor made a length-wise incision in her stomach downward from her naval. Then he made another incision in the uterus and delivered the baby that way. I won't go into all the details, but I feel this is the only way to save Victoria and the baby."

Marcus tried to still his trembling hands. "How dangerous is it?"

Dr. Spencer pushed his glasses up on his nose. "I won't lie to you, Marcus. I've never done this operation before. I don't think either the outside or inside incision will be hard to make, and I think we'll be able to get the baby out safely. I don't know about Victoria, however."

"You think she might die?" His voice was barely above a whisper.

"I don't know. Once I have the baby out, I will need to sew up both incisions. I don't know how long it will take me or how much blood she'll lose. But I do know this is the only option left to us."

Marcus sat still for a moment. He didn't want to think about having a baby without Victoria. But she was going to die if they didn't attempt the operation. He took a deep breath.

"Very well. I want you to do the operation."

Dr. Spencer nodded and pushed to his feet. "Do you want to talk to Victoria before I sedate her?"

Marcus jumped to his feet. "Yes."

He followed Dr. Spencer up the stairs and into the room once more. When he approached the bed, his heart lurched at her pale face. Her dark hair, matted from perspiration, fanned across the pillow. He knelt beside her, and Dr. Spencer stood on the other side of the bed.

"Victoria, can you wake up a moment?" he asked.

Her eyelids fluttered open, and she turned her head to stare at the doctor. "Yes."

He smiled and patted her arm. "It won't be long before your pain will be over. I've talked to Marcus, and we've decided you need an operation to deliver your baby. I'm going to put you to sleep so you won't feel anything. When you wake up, you'll have your baby. How does that sound?"

She licked her lips. "That makes me happy."

"I've also brought you a visitor. Marcus is here," he said.

She turned toward him and frowned. "Marcus? Is it you?"

"Yes, I'm here. Don't try to talk. Just rest. This is all going to be over soon."

She reached her hand up, and he grasped it. Her eyes blinked as if she had trouble focusing. "Is my mother here yet?"

"No, not yet. She'll be here soon, though, and she can hold her first grandchild."

She squeezed his hand tighter. "Tell her for me. . . ."

"What is it you want me to tell her?"

"That I love her. That I've always loved her."

A tear trickled from his eye. "You can tell her yourself when she gets here."

She closed her eyes and shook her head. "One more thing. Promise me."

"What? I'll promise you anything."

Pain flickered in her eyes as she looked up at him. "If I die, take care of our son. Don't teach him the things your father taught you. Listen to Dante and Daniel, and teach our child about God. Teach him to love all people. Will you do that?"

His chest felt as if his heart had shattered into pieces. "Don't talk like that, Victoria. We're going to raise our son together."

"No." She tried to push up in the bed, but he put his hand on her shoulders to restrain her. She lay back against the pillow and gasped. "Promise me you won't do to him what your father did to you. Promise me."

"I promise, Victoria. I promise." Tears ran down his cheeks.

She smiled and closed her eyes. "I love you, Marcus."

"I love you, too."

He pushed up from the bed and stumbled from the room. At the bottom of the steps, he spied the front door. He opened it and walked to the porch. As he walked toward them, the people rose from the quilts where they'd sat all night.

Tears ran down his face, but he didn't care. He faced the people whom Victoria loved. "Dr. Spencer is going to perform an operation to see if he can deliver the baby. He's never done this before. Please pray that God will be with him."

Without speaking, the people sat back down on the ground in silence. He looked around the group for a moment before he sat down on the ground next to James.

"Play your music for Victoria, James. Let her know how much she's loved."

James began to play, and the tune pierced his heart. Blues, Victoria had called James's music. It was first sung, she'd said, by the slaves as they reached out to God for deliverance. Now it filled his soul as he reached out to God and begged Him to spare his wife and child.

Thirty minutes later the front door opened, and Savannah ran onto the porch. "Marcus, come quick."

His heart pounding in his ears, he jumped up from the ground and raced to the porch. "What is it? Is Victoria all right?"

She smiled and motioned him into the house. "Dr. Spencer

is still working on Victoria, but there's someone you need to meet. Your son."

Sally stood at the bottom of the staircase, a blanket bundled in her arms. The blanket moved, and a shrill cry pierced the room. Marcus stumbled forward and stared down at the baby Sally held. He swallowed and looked up at her in disbelief. "Is this my son?"

She held the baby out to him. "Yas, suh. This heah yore baby. And he 'bout the purtiest one I ever seen."

Marcus reached for the baby but then thought better of it. "I've never held a baby before."

Dante and Daniel, who stood beside Sally, laughed. "You'd better get used to it," Dante said.

He attempted to control his shaking arms as he reached out and took the child in his arms. A feeling like he'd never experienced washed over him as he stared down at his son. From now on this child would depend on him, and he had made a promise to Victoria. No matter what happened, he intended to keep that promise.

He blinked back tears and smiled. "I want to go show him to all the people outside. There's a new life at Pembrook, and I want to share it with them."

Marcus tucked the blanket around the baby and stepped onto the front porch. "Dr. Spencer is still working with Victoria. So keep praying for her, but I want you to meet my son. Please step up here and see him."

The tenants looked from one to another as if they didn't know what to do. Ben and James stepped forward, and then the others followed. As they each came to look at the baby, Marcus felt for the first time that Pembrook was really beginning to feel like a home. Now all he needed to make it perfect was Victoria.

❧

Two months later on a hot August day, Victoria and Sally stood in the middle of the empty bedroom that had once been occupied by Marcus's father. Her mother had slept here during her visit, which had stretched from two weeks into two months. Now with her departure for Mobile, the time had come to convert the room into a nursery. Victoria glanced around the bare room. "Do you think we've missed anything, Sally?"

Sally propped her arm on the broom she held and shook her head. "No'm. I thinks it's all gone, and I'm glad. You been working too hard a-cleanin' this here room out. You still not well."

Victoria laughed. "How many times are you going to say that? I'm perfectly healed. Dr. Spencer said so."

"Well, he may be the doctor, but I doan knows that you needs to be doin' all this liftin' and cleanin'."

"You're beginning to sound like Marcus. The two of you would like to still have me in bed, but my son is now two months old. And I feel great."

Sally smiled. "He a real sweet baby."

Victoria nodded. "I think so, too. But I'm afraid Marcus is going to spoil him. He can't stay away from him."

"He gonna make a good daddy." Sally pointed to the marble-topped dresser that sat against the wall. "Did we gets ev'rythin' outta there?"

"I think so, but maybe we should check."

Victoria walked over to the dresser and pulled each of the drawers out one at a time. When she pushed the bottom one back in, she frowned and glanced at the decorative carving that ran across the very bottom of the piece of furniture. It appeared to be loose at the top. She put her fingers on the bottom of the carving and pulled it toward her to see if it held. To her surprise, the long piece of wood pulled forward to reveal a hidden drawer.

"Look at this," she called out. "There's a hidden drawer in the bottom of this dresser."

Sally moved behind her and stared over her shoulder as Victoria pulled the drawer all the way out. "Well, I done cleaned this here room a lot of times, and I never knowed there was no drawer there."

When Victoria had pulled it out as far as it would go, she stared down at the contents that appeared to be letters of some kind. She opened one, and her eyes grew wide at the signature scrawled at the bottom. Laying it down beside her, she scooped up the remaining letters and shuffled through them. There had to be at least a hundred in the drawer, and they were all from the same person.

Her hand shook, and she stared up at Sally. "Is Marcus in the barn?"

"Yes'm. He was a little while ago."

"Would you go get him and tell him I need to see him right away? It's an emergency."

Sally took one look at Victoria's face and bolted from the room. Within minutes Victoria heard Marcus's footsteps pounding on the staircase. Breathless, he ran into the room. "Sally said you needed me right away. What is it?"

She pointed to the letters scattered about her on the floor. "I found a secret drawer in your father's dresser. Inside were all these letters. Some of the older ones are addressed to your father. Some that are postmarked years later are addressed to you."

He frowned. "Letters to me? Who from?"

She held out her hand to him, and he walked to where she sat. "Oh, Marcus. They're from your mother."

His face paled, and he dropped to the floor beside her. "My mother? I. . .I don't understand. What do they say?"

"I don't know. They're for you to read first." She turned her head at the sound of the baby's cry. "I have to go feed the baby. Why don't you read them and tell me what they say?"

His lips trembled, and he glanced back down at the letters. "All right."

Victoria left the room and closed the door. As she walked to the bedroom where they'd placed the cradle for now, she prayed for her husband. She hoped words written by his mother years ago would at last bring healing to the wounds he'd suffered as a child.

Three hours later, however, Marcus still hadn't emerged from the room. She'd passed by the door several times and heard him walking about, but she hadn't wanted to disturb him.

She glanced out the kitchen window at the sun setting and wished he would come out. Sally had left for the day, supper was ready, and little Spencer lay on the pallet she'd placed in the corner of the room. She walked over to the baby she'd named after the doctor who'd saved their lives and picked him up.

"Have you been a good boy today?"

The baby gurgled, laughed, and squirmed in her arms.

"He's beautiful, isn't he?" Marcus's voice from the doorway startled her, and she looked up.

"Yes, he is." She waited for him to enter the room.

When he stepped nearer, she couldn't tell what he was feeling from the expression on his face. "I read the letters."

"And how do you feel?"

He raked his hand through his hair. "I don't know. I may struggle with that answer for a long time."

She took his hand and drew him toward the table. When

they were seated, she positioned the baby in her lap and turned to him. "Do you want to tell me about it?"

He nodded. "Yes. The first thing I learned is that my mother didn't leave Pembrook voluntarily. From her letters I gathered that my father was cold and cruel to her, not at all what she'd thought when they first met. He considered her his property and practically kept her isolated here. She wasn't allowed to go anywhere or have any friends. She was expected to cater to his every wish and be at his beck and call. Evidently if she didn't please him, he would lock her up for days at a time and was even abusive to her at times."

Victoria's heart broke with each word. "Oh no."

"Finally, she got up her nerve to tell him that she hated him and wanted to leave. She said she would take me and go back to her family. He accused her of being unfaithful to him and told her she would never see me again. He had the sheriff, who was a friend of his, come to Pembrook and drag her from the big house into a wagon that transported prisoners. Her letters were filled with hate for him at how she screamed and begged him to let her have me, but he laughed and slammed the door. The sheriff drove her to Selma and put her on a train to Montgomery. From there she traveled on to Boston, where her family lived."

Victoria reached across the table and grasped his hand. "Marcus, how awful. What about the letters to you?"

"As you know, she wrote those later. She said since I was older and could read, she hoped that some way one of them would fall into my hands. Most of them were written on my birthday, and she told me how much she loved me and that she was praying we'd see each other again someday."

Victoria frowned. "But the letters must have stopped at some time. I wonder why."

"I know why," he said. "The one with the last postmark was sent when I was about twelve years old. She wrote because my father had sent her a letter saying that I was killed in a riding accident. He even sent a copy of my death certificate."

"How could he get a death certificate for someone who was alive?"

"You didn't know my father. He could get anything he wanted. Anyway, that last letter was so sad. She told him that any link between them was gone, and he would never hear from her again. She ended by telling him that God was helping her cope with my death, and she could only pray that someday he would come to see how he'd ruined all our lives."

Marcus pushed up from the table and paced back and forth across the kitchen. He raked his hand through his hair. "How could he have been so cruel? He forced her to leave and then told me over and over how she didn't love me and didn't want to take me with her. I grew up without any love, and she was in Boston without me to love her back."

The baby stirred in her lap, and Victoria jiggled him around. "What are you going to do?"

He stopped in front of her, knelt, and wrapped his arms around both of them. "I'm so thankful that God's given you and Spencer to me, but there's a piece of me missing. After all these years, my mother may not be alive, but I have to find out. If she's still living, I have to bring her back here to see her grandson. Do you understand?"

Victoria smiled at him. "Of course I do. Go to Boston. Find your mother and bring her home."

fifteen

On a chilly October day Victoria waited inside the store that had belonged to her uncle until a year ago. She transferred Spencer from one arm to another and tried to smooth the wrinkles out of her skirt.

"Do I look all right?"

Savannah held out her hands to Spencer, who giggled and leaned toward the woman he knew so well. "How many times do we have to tell you that you look beautiful? Your mother-in-law is going to be so happy to see you that she won't care what you're wearing."

Tave, who stood on the other side of Victoria, chuckled. "You'd think royalty was coming with all the preparations you've been making."

"But I want her to feel good about coming back here. She left under such terrible circumstances. I want her to feel welcome."

Savannah bounced Spencer in her arms and smiled at him. She glanced at Victoria. "What did Marcus say in his letter?"

"He said he'd had a difficult time finding his mother. You know he's been in Boston for over a month. There was no one living at the address that was on the letters. It took him some time to find anyone in the neighborhood who had known the family or what happened to them. He went house to house in the area for days until he found a woman who'd been friends with his mother. She had an address where she thought he could find her."

Tave's eyes grew wide. "What happened when he went there?"

"A woman opened the door. He said for a moment he couldn't speak. Then he asked her if she was Elizabeth Raines. She told him she had been once but hadn't used the name in years. When he told her he was Marcus, she almost collapsed. From what he wrote, it was a very emotional reunion. And now she's coming back to live with us at Pembrook."

The low musical rumble of the *Montgomery Belle*'s whistle pierced the afternoon quiet, and the three women rushed to look out the door to the river landing. The tall smokestacks of the steamboat drifted into view, and Victoria reached for Spencer.

"They're here. Let's go."

Savannah jerked the door open. "Go on to the landing. You need to have a private meeting. We'll wait here for you."

Victoria held her son close and hurried across the street. She halted at the top of the bluff and watched as the big boat slid into its docking place and stopped. Within minutes the gangplank was lowered, and deck hands began to swarm ashore with baggage and goods.

Victoria scanned the decks for a glimpse of Marcus and his mother. Then she saw them. Marcus waved and leaned down to whisper to the woman beside him.

Marcus's mother looked small standing next to Marcus. Her head barely came to his shoulder. Her gray hair was pinned up underneath a wide-brimmed hat that matched the black traveling dress and coat she wore. Even from far away, Victoria could see the curling smile that reminded her so much of Marcus.

She watched as Marcus took his mother's arm and guided

her across the gangplank and up the bluff to the top of the landing. When they stopped in front of her, Marcus's eyes devoured her and Spencer before he turned back to his mother.

"Mother, this is my wife, Victoria, and my son, Spencer."

Victoria stepped closer. "Welcome home, Mother Raines. I can't tell you how happy I am you're here."

Tears flooded the woman's blue eyes as she looked from Victoria to Spencer. "Victoria, I understand I have you to thank for finding my letters of long ago."

Marcus leaned over, kissed Victoria on the cheek, and took Spencer from her arms. Victoria smiled at the frail woman facing her and grasped her hands. "I know you left under terrible circumstances and you've had years to think about it. But I've prayed that you can let all of that go and enjoy being here. We want you to be a part of our family and share the love that lives at Pembrook now."

"When I left Alabama, I prayed I would see my son again someday, but that hope was destroyed when I thought he'd died. Now God has answered my prayer of long ago."

"You're home now, and that's all that matters," Victoria said.

Marcus handed Spencer back to Victoria. "I want the three of you to stand there for just a moment."

He walked a few steps from the landing and turned to face them. Victoria and her mother-in-law exchanged questioning glances. Victoria tilted her head to one side and stared at him. "What are you doing, Marcus?"

"I was just thinking how quickly one's life can change. A year and a half ago, I stood right here and watched a beautiful woman get off a steamboat. That woman is now my wife. I have a son. And today I have the mother I've wanted for years. God has brought a lot of blessings to me on this river."

Marcus came toward them, his arms outstretched, and drew the three of them close. "I never thought I could be so happy. God has blessed me more than I ever could have imagined."

Victoria stood on tiptoe and kissed her husband's cheek. "You're right. God has been good to us. I think we're going to have to teach James some new songs. There aren't going to be any blues around Pembrook from now on."

A Letter To Our Readers

Dear Reader:

In order that we might better contribute to your reading enjoyment, we would appreciate your taking a few minutes to respond to the following questions. We welcome your comments and read each form and letter we receive. When completed, please return to the following:

Fiction Editor
Heartsong Presents
PO Box 719
Uhrichsville, Ohio 44683

1. Did you enjoy reading *Blues Along the River* by Sandra Robbins?

❑ Very much! I would like to see more books by this author!

❑ Moderately. I would have enjoyed it more if

_____

_____

_____

2. Are you a member of **Heartsong Presents**? ❑ Yes ❑ No
   If no, where did you purchase this book? _____

_____

3. How would you rate, on a scale from 1 (poor) to 5 (superior), the cover design? _____

4. On a scale from 1 (poor) to 10 (superior), please rate the following elements.

____ Heroine   ____ Plot
____ Hero   ____ Inspirational theme
____ Setting   ____ Secondary characters

5. These characters were special because? _____

_____

_____

6. How has this book inspired your life? _____

_____

_____

7. What settings would you like to see covered in future
   Heartsong Presents books? _____

_____

_____

8. What are some inspirational themes you would like to see
   treated in future books? _____

_____

_____

9. Would you be interested in reading other **Heartsong
   Presents** titles? ❏ Yes ❏ No

10. Please check your age range:
    - ❏ Under 18   ❏ 18-24
    - ❏ 25-34   ❏ 35-45
    - ❏ 46-55   ❏ Over 55

Name _____

Occupation _____

Address _____

City, State, Zip _____

E-mail _____